The Way to Liberation

The Way to Liberation

Debabrata Madanray

Translated by
Brajamohan Mishra

BLACK EAGLE BOOKS
DUBLIN, USA | ODISHA, INDIA

BLACK EAGLE BOOKS

USA address:
7464 Wisdom Lane
Dublin, OH 43016

India address:
E/312, Trident Galaxy, Kalinga Nagar,
Bhubaneswar-751003, Odisha, India

E-mail: info@blackeaglebooks.org
Website: www.blackeaglebooks.org

First International Edition Published by
BLACK EAGLE BOOKS, 2025

THE WAY TO LIBERATION
by **Debabrata Madanray**

Translated by **Brajamohan Mishra**

Original Copyright © **Debabrata Madanray**
Translation Copyright © **Brajamohan Mishra**

Cover & Interior Design: Ezy's Publication

ISBN- 978-1-64560-704-5 (Paperback)

Printed in United States of America

For
Anand & Sourabh

Contents

FOREWORD

It goes without saying that translation (especially literary translation) is an act of love. At times, one is magnetised by a literary work and if one is a perceptive literary artist, one is impelled to translate it. In fact, Debabrata Madanray's stories hypnotised this translator so much that he felt possessed to translate those immortal creations. Rightly has opined Prof. K.R. Srinivas Iyengar, 'The good short story is always a reflection of a chosen slice of life; but it is also, sometimes a warning, and sometimes a prophecy - a warning of craters ahead, or an invitation to Pisgah heights of Possibility.'- *(The Adventure of Criticism-P 162)*. Applying this yardstick to Madanray's stories, a sensible reader can safely and surely hold that his stories entertain and enlighten because of their philosophic magnitute, superb ambience of style and fidelity to experience.

December 20, 2024   **Brajamohan Mishra**

AUTHOR'S NOTE

Indeed the world of story is stupendous. Whenever I have entered it, I have been delightfully awestruck and transported to an empyrean. Moreover, I have felt overwhelmed whenever I have spoken something about it. Modern Odia short story has reached its 126th year bearing stories of three generations. Varied experiments on the style, language, dramatic elements, features of the short story as a literary genre are being done. I am participating in it. Modern Odia short story is a delectable pageantry; it is more individual and theme-centred.

My literary journey is of four decades. I have been meditative on the opulence of prospective words. My book *Mokhya Patha* has been translated into English and is going to be published. While reading, the reader will feel that he himself is a character whose life has been told. I have X-rayed the pageantry of the individual; have portrayed the rainbow of a higher flight. The stream of stories is noble-strange are its pictures, characters, and incidents.

I am very much grateful to Brajamohan Mishra for his translation and valuable suggestions. Translating my Odia stories into English, he has presented them to readers. I shall be glad if the book is cordially received.

December 20, 2024   Debabrata Madanray

Mahatma

Utmost mute was the sky, the wind howling. Everybody turned speechless. None should be such obdurate slighting others' persuasion. An insulting scene for the teacher. In spite of repeated persuasion Prashant insisted to play the role of Gandhiji on the independence day to be observed after three days. The teacher had selected a weak boy to play the role. He fell ill and remained absent. The teacher expressed this in the prayer class. Thereafter Prashant came foreward and said, 'Sir, I shall play the role.'

The teacher got disgusted with the unsavage and painful spectacle. However, Prashant didn't budge. He did not request for this rather he was prepared for a showdown. The teacher's face presented his conflict and helplessness. The fact was Prashant used to simulate a tiger every year. The human face would remain hidden behind the mask he put on. And when he would jump wagging tail he would appear to be a real tiger.

A stockily built young boy, he would put on iron bangles. Consequently children would be scared and keep distance. And the moment he would gnash his teeth and step forward, they would move away from his tail. Indeed, his tail and claws would look more terrible than his teeth.

'All right. You would play the role of Gandhi' - the teacher expressed this not to stretch the fixed time of prayer.

Students present were taken aback. They failed to fathom why the teacher agreed so easily. A sense of incomprehension was writ large on their faces. But Prashant's face glistened with a ray of laughter like that of a tiger. The iron bangles in his hands glistened in soft sunshine.

A little while later the teacher said, 'Well, but on a condition.'

It created a strange moment. Prashant had never thought he would have to abide by a condition to play the role of Gandhiji.

He asked in a low voice, 'What condition?'

In fact, the teacher was waiting for this. Closing eyes he said, 'You shouldn't tell lies for two days.'

An easy condition to keep. Prashant got delighted . He nodded his head in agreement - what to speak of not saying lies for two days, he won't tell lies at all even for three days. His face exuded a suppressed laughter - who could know whether or not he told a lie? Do all children speak the truth? Telling lies is a trifle.

'No, not like that, you have to speak out loudly' - The teacher commanded him.

But the students present were sure he could not do so; surely he would fumble the moment he spoke out loudly before them. He would promise to speak untruth instead of truth. However, it didn't come about. Prashant uttered the words distinctly, 'I will speak the truth.' Then he wiped his face with his hand. His lips were trembling a bit - he perceived. Yet he controlled himself to the best of his capability. There was enough possibility for his being stupefied. He couldn't believe he agreed to such a condition at last.

The teacher chuckled. He approached Prashant and

told him mildly, 'Have you seen the images of three monkeys kept on my table?'

What do the idols cannote? Is it so very essential to see them? I shall be Gandhiji but why should I see those three idols? Prashant expressed indignantly.

- No, sir.

The teacher kept smiling. His smile was pregnant with esotericism. All students waited for his next question.

- Meet me after the class is over. The teacher bade Prashant which startled all. They turned quizzical - may be the teacher felt unable to give vent to his annoyance and anger before all. Certainly he would belch it when Prashant was alone.

The teacher's eyes looked more pacified, more mysterious.

While walking along the verndah Prashant felt ruffled.

A lot of flowers had bloomed here and there - red, black and yellow. Some flowers got scattererd on the clean verndah making it unclean. A paper rocket started flying in the class room and then fell near the blackboard. It was Prashant's rocket that had crossed a long distance.

Prashant laughed uproariously. He had won because of his insistence. He never won a prize in the prize giving ceremony as he played the role of a tiger. His tiger-dance, though performed proudly, was unable to fetch him any award. Why should one give away a prize to a boy playing such a role? Even a boy weaker than him used to win prize, praise. Thus he would smile triumphantly before all. The teacher also used to place his hand on his shoulder affectionately. What more could be a matter of honour than this?

It was Prashant's final class in the school. Nobody could say where his classmates would study after the matriculation examination. So what harm if he was praised playing once the role of Gandhiji ?

A minister would be invited to the meeting and appear more majestic due to TV people's presence. On a lighted pandal the minister would present him a bouquet and a citation. Why should he lose such an opportunity? Let somebody else play the role of a tiger. That would be the teacher's decision.

Prashant was full of excitemet. After the last class, he stalked to the teacher like a tiger. Looked at the table sharply. The three monkey statues were unmoved.

The teacher took pity on his ignorance and said, 'Well, what significance the statues inhere! They indicate that nobody should speak evil, see evil and hear evil. Gandhiji himself had experimented with this truth.'

Prashant's excitement got worn off so soon which he had not imagined.

He couldn't ask his teacher, 'Should he know Gandhian philosophy to play the role of Gandhiji on the independence day?' Because no such realization was so important for him at that moment.

The teacher handed him over a green packet. Startled, he looked at it - what did the packet contain? Some books on Gandhian philosophy? He had no time at all to go through such Gandhian books. He would return all such - he thougt.

The teacher nonchalantly said, 'A piece of cloth, a cotton chadar and spactacles for you. Put on these articles and rehearse for three days. Lest you won't be able to walk like Gandhiji. You would stumble. I shall be happy if you can walk as Gandhiji used to walk. I have hardly found a person living with his philosophy. I bless you. You could accomplish it.'

Prashant was taken aback. Very naturally. He had never expected to experience such a moment.

Trembled from top to toe. Felt unconscious, as it were everything - the room, the world at large - seemed immobile.

While he was about to leave the room, Prashant heard his teacher saying, 'Do you remember, you shouldn't lie?'

- Yes, Sir, replied he.

- For three days.

As he reached the verndah, some change in his walk surfaced. He was walking slightly bent. A sort of faith was heavily put on his shoulder, as it were. He had forgotten to walk like a tiger.

A scene such as this was strange and accidental. Some of the flowers had already lost their freshness. In such an environment of freshness a bird, perched on a branch of a tree, flew.

He met with a pitiable scene when he reached home. Father was loitering inside . As though he would smash almirah, cot, table, etc. Consequently, articles would get scattered. He was quite restless. He shouted, 'How come some money was stolen when so many persons were present at home! And none of you could know ! Strange! Be off, be off. Get out of my house.'

Whenever he would get angry, he used to lose self-control. He would be unable to know what he said. He used to spend his anger at mother. Prashant didn't know how his father could become so energetic. Mother would keep mum as she knew father was able to manage house in the teeth of wants.

- Have you seen? I had kept money to pay your school fees; here in this almirah.

His last three words made mother doubtless. She knew

at times father would forget where he kept things. And he would ransack the house. Last year he kept the lease deed on the almirah but searched trunks and bookshelves.

'Have you taken? Tell me.' - Mother asked me in low tone. Just at that time was seen at the other side of the door, sister's tearful face. Last night she proposed to witness a film. We had no money. What could be done? She opened the almirah and said father won't be able to know if some money was pilfered.

Her confidence showed them the way to steal.

Prashant felt puzzled - what would he say? Father asked again, 'Have you seen who has taken?'

A moment frightened and insulted, as it were-awaited on the otherside of the door. If he answered yes, he could cross the threshold and enter the house. But it was unusual. He was vanquished inside. Then he said, 'How can I know? I returned from school. Might be you have given it somebody but fail to remember.'

Dejected, father sat on the cot.

Prashant looked at him, thought he should speak something more. But he realised he had spoken untruth.

At least half an hour elapsed in silence. Prashant felt unable to put up with it. Anxiety ridden, he paddled his bicycle keeping his notes and books in its carrier and crossed the gate. He had no time to repent.

He felt terribly hungry after the tuition was over. They might dine in any hotel, fried salad he suggested. He was unable to agree. Mother must have waited for him. If he turned late a little, father be pacing to and from the gate. Sister must have sat near the window. He declined.

Exasperated, Subodh said, 'Why behaving like a eunuch? It won't be much late. We would return after dining after half an hour.'

Prashant found three other persons. As though they had waited for him! They shook hands, didnot speak. An offlid bottle lay in their front. Wine had been served in glasses and meat in three plates. He had never thought of encountering a situation like this.

Wiping his perspering face with his palm, he said, 'At home mother must have waited for me.'

Subodh pressed his shoulder down and made him seated.

One of the three present there said, 'I have seen this boy before. He dances the tiger- dance excellently. He should join our party. Before he joins college, he needs to be trained in the art of launching movement, agitation and bund.'

Prashant stared at him.

' Well, nobody falls if he/she takes meat and drinks casually. Gandhiji too had drunk. We are sure you could be a person in political chessboard. Your father controls so many voters. We must get those at the time of election.'

Prashant was getting excited inside. Even though he wiped sweat time and again, it glistened on his forehead. What harm if he drank a draught to get rid of such a situation? He won't be ruined as his father said at times. Who cares!

Out of the hotel, Prashant failed to walk straight . Subodh seated him on his bicycle. Though the handle swerved this side and that, Prashant kept rules of the road. The breeze was blowing amid the foliage of mango trees.

In darkness father was waiting for him at the gate.

Prashant got off the bicycle and placed all burden against the wall.

- What has happened to you? Where had you been?

Who else returns so late at night! We have been waiting. I admit I got annoyed with you. But why do you mind it so much? Get angry and sulky and return home wandering here and there! Father's words, almost inaudible, were soaked in tears.

Prashant could not reply. May be he had no power to do so. He explained as if he had lost everything. Hiding his face, he went inside the house, put out the lamp and fell asleep. That was the only easy way for him to alleviate feelings of pain and defeat.

He woke up to a disciplined dawn. He found his note, book kept arranged on the table. His pen and geometry box were there too. So was the unopened packet of green colour.

He was not interested to anything more. Somehow he opened the packet. Put on dhoti, slightly upturned. As it covered upto his knees, he covered his body with a chadar in a dishevelled manner and wore spectacles.

Before the mirror he discovered himself to be a different man. That figure could be counted as Gandhiji's. He should hold a long piece of stick in hand. The stick placed against the wall could serve the purpose. Thinking so, he walked to the wall; he met his mother. His eyes were swollen, face looked pale; was he sleepless last night?

Prashant could not excuse himself for the incident happened last night.

- Hay, tell me the truth. Where had you been last night? Your father smelled odour of wine on your face - she said.

Prashant was perturbed, felt he was defenceless, as it were.

- Rubbish! all lies. Father has lost mental power. Since he is launching anti-liquor agitation, he smells wine everywhere. You need not stress his words -he said.

Mother left for the other room.

Prashant told a lie, indeed. Distancing himself safely, he was surprised but felt frightened - unable to speak the truth though he had dressed himself like Gandhiji. It was impossible on his part to muster courage to do so.

Quite natural it was that he was shaken inside. He reached school and felt enervated. His yesterday's defiance was no more with him.

After the prayer class, he met the teacher, who chuckled.

- What happened? Have you started walking like Gandhiji? he asked.

Prashant wept inconsolably uncontrollably. As if his inner world ruined! He deposited the greenpacket on the table, folded his hands and said, 'Failed. Failed to speak the truth. I am afraid, may be I have learnt to speak the untruth only. I thought wearing spectacles you had given me I might not appear like Gandhiji, but I should have looked like my father. But that was not to be . Even I failed to recognise myself before the mirror. How could I look like Gandhiji?'

The teacher smiled and said, 'Looking like Gandhiji and be Gandhiji - two different matters. Is it so easy to be Mahatma?

That's why I made conditions for you to observe. But as I hear you now you have sprouted new hopes in me. You will comprehend Gandhian philosophy, apply it in life - if not today, then tomorrow.'

You may have been deeply puzzled after hearing a lot about Prashant. May be you think it to be a story. But it is true, Prashant was my classmate. I am that weak boy our teacher had chosen to play the role of Gandhiji. The teacher called for me after Prashant had declined. I was suffering from fever. Yet I played the role on the Independence Day. Stood first in competition as I used to be every year.

My eyes rolled here and there while I received prizes on the stage. But he was not there. He had not played the role of a tiger. Nobody could know why he did so - whether out of sulk or helplessness.

Results of our matriculation examination were amazing beyond measures. Prashant bagged the second position among the best ten positions. He missed the first position for short of ten marks.

He accommodated himself with his relative at Bhubaneswar and prosecuted his studies there. I did my studies at Cuttack. At times we had chances to meet when I marked him to be grave and more composed.

After studies I taught in a college at Raygada. Completing post graduation, he headed for Delhi, sat for the UPSC examination. Clicked IAS. That was a very important peice of news for our area published in newspapers.

Somedays later a similar amazing news came out - a senior IAS officer's request to the government for voluntary retirement though he had five more years to be in service.

I was wonder-struck. What an extraordinary and unusual dicision! I got curious to know if he would join any political party after such decision.

May be .

Prashant's way of life had expanded.

He said very slowly, 'After joining service I met our teacher at school three to four times. Everytime he spoke to me about the philosophy of Gandhi - whenever you do any work, remember the visage of the poorest and weakest man and think whether your work should benefit him. If yes, do that.'

- Then what was your difficulty? You have done so much for the poor of our area. That's why you are famous.

Yet why did you opt for voluntary retirement? You can render service only when you are in service.' I said.

He paused for a while and said, 'I was defeated. I didn't concur with a government project, declined to put my signature. Because I could know such a project would not benefit the poorest. Rather it would salivate so many wealthy persons.'

In fact, Prashant was not defeated. On the other hand, he was victorious for his ideal, though he didn't put on Gandhiji's spectacles. Without putting it on, he was able to read Gandhian philosophy. Only our teacher could have said how many persons did really derive contentment when they retired.

The Way to Liberation

Tendrils of pumpkin have spread on the thatched roof . Earthen walls all around. A verndah appeared like a handful of affection embedded in faith. An earthen hearth touched the verndah. A solitary moonlit night upon the hearth. The moon beams were resplendent in the wallniche. The shadow of a drum hanging from the wooden beam appeared clear on the wall not so clean. Yet everything was alienated, unsheltered.

Mother said in a dispassionate tone to hammer the solitary house, 'Does the house count? Would he come back even if you kept the house spruce and intact?'

Indeed a gush of sigh hid unending trials and tribulations.

A citrus decumana tree stands adjacent to the wall. Its fruits, when ripe, used to scatter its flavour all around. Children returning from school would get clamorous, the surrounding turning crowded. They would relish the juice of ripe citrus decumana that streamed down their lips. All with loud laughter. They were unware of an inversion - an open, well-broken rings of stone put around it. In the long run the tree was felled with an axe. It crashed with its branch just at a litte distance, beneath the bauhima tree.

Mother stood motionless. Could cross the wall. But a silent competition between the sun and the moon used to go on to prove between the two who was lucky.

After the citrus decumena tree was felled, children returning from school, flocked to the embankment of the tank. They would throw their satchels there and engage in playing on water with potshreds. The salient feature of the game was how long the potsherds could proceed on water. In course of the game, drops of water would get scattered by the wind and the tank would glow in amazing beauty. Countless silver coins fell from heaven, as it were . For a while, Sania glanced at those glistening drops of water and said, 'A ghost inhabits your house. It beats drum in midnight when the wind wheezes, carrying the tinkling sound of bangles.'

I bent myself to look into the tank. To find where silver coins fell. I didn't look at him and spoke breathlessly, 'That is not our house. That belongs to our junior grandfather, dead long since. I have n't seen him.'

The matter would be over - I thought. But Sania looked at him disgustingly. Perhaps he knew something secret. He might ask me about its truth after a while, "Your younger grandfather had brought a beautiful damsel from Berhampur. She was much younger. Her bangles tinkled in dark night. Do you know? While returnig from the market last night Jadua happened to meet her in the middle of the road.'

The house has never encountered a moment of adversity. However, it required yearly repair . Adept hands repairing it would throw away rotten straws on the roof and replace carefully bunches of straw of golden hue. They were so arranged as to appear like a golden wrapper woven at and brougt from paddy fields. Then there would be no apprehension of sun and rain. Father, therefore, was not interested to pull the house down.

The shadow of the drum spread all over the wall.

Someone resided there. And the shadow was half-bent not to reveal his indentity, as it were. That's why, the vermilion lines on the wall were vanishing by degrees. While cleaning it was almost dubious that a broken bangle could come to sight. Similarly there was no responsibility of the sound of an idle foot coming out to the village road. But whenever someone expressed in trepidation that he had heard drum beating, father on the verndah, would dismiss it as 'false' a number of times the like chanting of an incantation.

Mother used to hear this but keep mum, though she would get frightened a little. She would collect sacred water from our prayer room and sprinkle throughout our house to avert any untoward incident. That indicated the house, segregated totally, was a secret area inaccessible to all. Though adjacent to our house area none had access to cross its wall. Yet the sun and the moon used to compete with each other to ascertain who was more fortunate.

Solitary were the surroundings. I felt someone crossed me along with the wind, as it were. I picked up my satchel and ran homeward. Reached home. Couldn't believe I could run so fast! May be the wind and time run so.

Mother wiped my sweating face. She appeared unhappy, her face contorted with wrinkles. May be she knew of the incident last night. Such encounter on the village road was not at all insignificant.

- 'Have you seen?'
- 'Whom?'

No more could I muster courage. Nor did I know the necessity of asking such a question.

Mother's eyes glistened with tears. She appeared to be an ordinary statue. I didn't know of a statue's mobility. But mother could visualise the inside of the house-wall, verndha, etc. As she proceeded towards the verndah, she muttered, 'I have asked her time and again to demolish the house but of no avail.'

Her words had an indistinct meaning, Thought I, the matter must be travelling throughout the village this way. Father may have harboured hope that younger grandma would return to that house someday . Like a person finding his way.

But she didn't as expected. Father's prayer came to naught.

Was there a conspiracy which grandma was unable to overcome and return then? Mother got obsessed with this anxious thought that contributed to the mystery of the house.

The house was locked. Even the wind didn't venture to cross its threshold. However, some wind hovered inside in quest, as it were .

It was time for matriculation exam. Father was reluctant to allow me to prepare for the exam inside it .

- How can that be? Let the house stand as it is. It has been awaiting her return. She would mark it on her return' He said.

The house ramained locked up. Yet sunshine and untimely rain never ceased enjoying shelter on its verndah. Who could impede them? I only remember hazily a rare scene, a cat jumping on the wall and entering an insurmountable house.

Time floats in the stream of the wind. The yard of bamboos has disappeared. Buildings have been built in the village. Now the villagers are getting hypnotised by Surat. Their be all and end all is earning. More earning yields more happiness. On the other hand, the possibility of enjoying a scene of the village road getting crowded with religious festivals. Roads widened have been connected with the National Highway. If one falls ill, one no more goes to Pattamundai. Straightway one heads towards Cuttack. There is a big medical. Treatment of all diseases is available there.

No more is the village alienated. No more does it suffer from hunger, fatigue, uncertainty. A water tank stands there like a big banyan tree. Each house is getting pipe water. The burial ground has shifted farther fearfully. Not to lose its indentity beside the narrow water course. Now the village road is spick and span. Darksness at night has disappeared due to electric light. None needs to shout in darkness to know anyone's identity.

The unforeseen incident took place in such an apathetic, and enduring time. While returning from school, father fell off the bicycle. Sustained deep forehead injury. Blood-drenched were his face and shirt. I failed to indentify his blood stained face when he reached home. Tears in her eyes, mother stood against the wall. I felt diffident to approach her.

However, father was conscious. Before I asked him he said gently, 'Don't worry. I am ok.All on a sudden a cow ran to the road. So I pulled the brake, thus fell down. Only my face has smashed against boulders heaped there for road construction.'

These words strengthened me. I thought the situation was not that terrible. Nothing would get alienated - the earth or the sky.

'Give way to the doctor' - Someone said . The doctor appeared grave as he had put on specs of thick- lens. He cleared blood stains from father's face with a piece of cotton soaked in dettol. The wound on the face became visible. Now the doctor anointed ointmnent. He bandaged the wound and then brought out a syringe from his bag. Father had no reaction when the injection was pricked. The doctor gave me two strips of medicine and said, 'Not a serious injury; I prescribe medicine for five days. If the injury persists , I shall advise taking medicine for two more days.'

While saying these the doctor appeared conscious of the dress he had puton. In fear of his dress getting soiled, he didn't sit in the chair. Very slowly he said, 'I have a lot to do in my clinic.'

I looked around. The crowd got thinned as the doctor departed. But I felt anxiety growing in me. A state of helplessness indeed. God knew why in me a sense of fear got coagulated.

- Can you raise your right hand? I asked.

Father's eyes indicated a sign of debilitation and dread.

Someone's hand touched my shoulder. I looked back. He was our priest - a sandal paste mark on forehead and a white towel spread on his shoulder.

A little pause later, he said , 'That man from Midnapur is an ignoramus - but has opened a clinic! Indeed he is a compounder. But he poses as a doctor. Litsten to me. Admit your father at Cuttack. It's head injury. Who knows what will happen?'

At such a moment of adversity one needed consolation, solace. None was there to guide me with assuring words - be sure, things will be all right. Certainly he will come round if admitted to Cuttack medical. Then he will return to village and loiter around paddy fields. He will be overwhelmed with joy while enjoying the paddy fields of ripecorn.

Mother was sobbing inside the house. The bicycle was put against the wall - its handle of faded colour, mudguard pressed inside, its carrier slightly bent, and a cotton bag hanging.

- I studied Adikanda's horoscope two days back. The planet saturn is on ascendant. I advised him to be careful and chant the Mahamrutyunjayan mantra and worship Lord with bel-leaves. So that the adversity could be averted.

I was shattered inside; my eyes got bedimmed with tear and grief. Gradually I was becoming enervated. I appeared pathetic.

The priest looked at the cloudy sky and departed.

I held father's left hand and lifted him slowly. A very sturdy person but now unable to stand straight on his legs. He leaned on me.

Two tablets and a glass of milk. - enough for his diet at night.

Speechless, he fell asleep leaning to one side.

I felt bedevilled and suffocated. As if I shall be lifeless just now.

The morning sky ws not cloudy. But cloudy were the entire house and mother's heart. Tears gushed not from her eyes but from her heart. She was unable to wail. Asleep, father had departed . Very easily and without informing any one a little. He appeared to respond at once and get up; take bath, pray in the room of worship; take a little food and start for school riding the bicycle kept against the wall.

But all in vain, all unreal, false. May he breathe again - No. Darkness in the night had swallowed all our happiness. Assuring my mind, notwithstanding, his heart didn't beat. His body lay cold.

What a moment! The person didn't respond even if he was called loudly. Everything got stupefied. As though all doors closed!

There was commotion on the road outside. It got stretched upto the funeral ground. The corpse was clad in a new piece of cloth and laid on the pyre. There were flowers, sandal wood, ghee and fire to lit the pyre. Enough to burn into ashes the lac house of relationship, appearing invincible.

All will be immortal and indestructible. Such connotation was not true. Rather a false aphorism.

The priest performed obsequies chanting slokas and putting betelnut and unboiled rice on a plantain leaf. He looked pale and dispassionate - the surroundings looked melancholic.

In spite of this strange morning, a scene that had not been seen during the last twenty years was seen. Apparently such a moment was speechless and antimidating altogether.

A grown up lady, full of eagerness, crossed the verndah , entered the house and stood humbly at the threshold. Her eyes shone like a fine dawn. She had put on a saree of champak flower colour and a garland of the holy basil plant

Taken aback,and sobbing, mother uttered, 'Auntie.'

Who was that old lady?

Mother couldn't restrain her passion for union with her any more. She touched her feet and said, ' Alas! you returned after he departed!' Mother's sobbing made the atmosphere more pathetic. Yet friends and relatives present couldn't believe the appearance of the lady at such a time of adversity. Why was she present? When others felt uncomfortable because of her presence, mother caught hold of her hand like her kith and kin.

Younger grandma stayed for three days. She appeared nonchalant as if she had not lost anything. Every evening she would read a chapter from the Bhagabat. She spoke to none except mother. But her demeanour registered a sense of quest. What for was her quest? On the fourth day morning she said to mother, 'I shall leave to-day. Will you please take me into that house?'

A request humbly expressed. Not at all a claim. Rather it was a humble expression to meet safely some reminiscences.

A bird chirped at a door somewhere. Even though the lock was opened after a long time, there was no garbage in the house. Only a few dry leaves had fallen on the verndah.

I stood behind mother.

Crossing the verndah, the younger grandma approached the niches on the wall, pulled out something from it. What was that? A moment of utter amazement. A gush of cold air shot through the front door.

Younger grandma held an idol of Lord Jagannath. A divine experience spread throughout the room. It was not easy to admit on any one's part to claim the ownership of that room. A jerking sound was heard and the front door got shut by the wind.

Things seemed uncanny. Mother stood transfixed. How come, she failed to see the idol so long! The black idol of rinkless round eyes; bewitching smile. Mother got enmeshed in an invisible net, as though.

Embellished with dry sandal paste and a garland of holy basil, our younger grandma exuded a mysterious smile. Gently she said, 'I had set out for Puri from Berhampur. On the midway your younger father in law magnetised me. He was playing a drum and singing devotional songs of Jagannath. I accompanied him to this house and stayed here. He had assured me to leave me at Puri.'

Like a child she clasped the Lord's idol to her bosom. I asked myself, 'Who can hold the Lord like this!' Without hiding any matter, she continued, 'He was ok. But in the night he screamed clasping his belly. God knows what the matter was. It rained cats and dogs and I was alone. Our verndah was flooded. Even rain water touched our threshold. I thought to do something at the dawn. But the scream was heard no more. Perhaps he fell asleep, I thought. He passed away that night. Looking at his dead body, I prayed to Lord Jagannath.'

- I came to you in the morning and knew he was no more. But why did you leave the place in such a manner without informing anybody and hiding your face? - Mother asked calmly.

The question made desperation on yonger grandma's face evident. She said in a low tone, 'What else could have I done? How long could have I hidden myself in that dark room? I thought it wiser to leave the village than hear someone tapping on the closed window in darknight. Hence I closed the door and left. However, I put the responsibilities of the deity on Adikanda's shoulder. He also assured to adorn the deity with flowers and worship everyday. I dreamt a strange dream before four to five days. The Lord said to me, I have remained unworshipped in your house. So I hastened to this place and saw Adikanda absent.'

Time stood still.

Stupefied, mother looked at younger grandma and wanted to hear what more she would speak. But she failed to say anything, caressed the idol of Jagannath in tearful eyes.

I was unable to understand why such a person was crying.

- Why did you not participate in obsequies? Mother asked her gently.

Suddenly younger grandma's face got contented. Very

clearly she said, 'Had I married him?' Does a person whose home is Srimandir, need any other worldly family?'

Time appeared so lively, so moving. She moved onward with a faith that Jagannath was her companion, as it were.

The Lion's Gate was in her front; so were the twenty-two steps

Incantation of the Woods

Kankadahada was decided at last to be their destination. From Delhi will come Sumanta and from Benaras, Ajay. They never met me after they had retired. The dam at Dandadhar is located at Kankadahada; its water crystalline. They determined to spend some moments in the dense sal jungle there.

After post graduation, Sumanta headed for Delhi to live with his brother and prepare for IAS. However, he failed in the first chance. But his second attempt didn't nullify his desire. He joined the Rajstan cadre, spent most of his service period outside Odisha. But whenever he came to Odisha, he did not fail to meet me. Nobody can deny his interest to know about the Orissan political climate. After retirement he was staying in Delhi where he had built a house much earlier. His only son was in America.

Ajay, too, didn't come back. After teaching in Ravenshaw for some years, he joined BHU. Retired as Professor of English. Like so many people, he chose Benaras as his domicile. He was infatuated with the Ganges. His wife was a Professor there and his only daughter was prosecuting her studies there too. I felt uncomfortable to lead a rootless life. So I stayed there. Before completion of my studies I had joined Bank service. I served at many places in Odisha and now I am at Kamakhyanagar branch. Shall retire next month.

I didn't like to live elsewhere. Not that I lacked opportunities. But the smell of my native place overwhelmed me. I got tied to a whiff of air, a portion of the sky. I am there where I was. That's my whereabouts and my indentity as well.

Though I spent so many days here that scene exclusively doesn't get obliterated from my memory. At times I ask myself what is that scene constituted of? Is it more beautiful than flower, the sky and cloud or more colourful than the rainbow? Is it so essential to lead a life of fulfilment? However, they have enjoyed such an existence. But why, at this ripe age, he was so eager to meet Saraswati? Did they not know about this beforehand?

Saraswati - beautiful; her eyes glistening, her lips slightly red; hair cascaded against her shoulders. Her veil flaping in the wind. The wind would also turn restless when she crossed the gate and entered the college campus. It would touch her lips, brow and body; her veil would fall down. So that it was quite natural on her part to arrange her veil with her fingers. This scene fixed a definition of living a life fulfilled and would be capable to extend the base of catholic lovc.

Someone says at that time - Where were you so long? The campus sans your presence appears desolate. Come, stand beside me under the tree. Even if you donot touch me, the wind which touched you would touch me.

A very overwhelming moment indeed when the wind blows.

Though none but I could hear I knew Sumant said so. In silence he stood beneath the tree and gazed at the sky. He would turn into a tiger if he got an opportunity - claws would grow; clasping with sharp teeth he would drag his prey into a jungle. The surroundings would be terrible , leaves would appear red.

In fact, passion is terrible and its colour is red. Ajay would be waiting in the classroom. There would be load shedding. Hence the colour of the veil wouldn't be visible. Saraswati herself would be unable to know of the colour of the veil she had put on. Then it would rain and the surroundings would get dark. How could one recognise the colour in rain water! The face would be smeared with mud and the body drenched in water.

There would be no colour, no painter's brush. Yet the portrait would be drawn.

This may sound irrelevant to you. - Is it possible? Skirmishes occur almost at each college election. Nothing new now. Sanjay contested for the post of president. His face on the banner looked unusually grave. He was backed by a political party. Hence money was being spent on the campus lavishly. Feast everyday. Nobody could infer it bred all types of danger. None could apprehend that the auditorium, would be a battleground.

Everything was rent after the results of the election were declared. Torn pieces of banner flew in the sky. Rims of bicycles were bent with iron rods. Seats on bicycles were made loose. While someone's head got wounded, some other's hand got beaten teribbly. Sanjay was shouting loudly. The brass ring he had worn indicated his wrath. It was a terrible moment of running here and there.

Sanjay lost mental balance. He knew it very well it was a very easy way to register a protest.

He was possessed by an evil spirit, as it were. He had no courage to swallow defeat. Jingling of window panes being broken made the enviromment more terrifying.

He was defeated in spite of all possibility of victory. How could he withstand such a crisis? His defeat alienated him completely from the political party he belonged to. He was perturbed. What would he do now? Indeed, he was unable to prove his superiority.

As Sanjay entered the classroom the room turned silent. All its relationship with the wellknown world got snapped, as it were!

Sporting a cosmetic smile he asked, 'Did you cast your vote in my favour?' It was not a mere question rather a threat that portened the things to come. Everything was petrified. Saraswati was sitting in the front row. Sumanta and Sanjay sat in the row behind her and I sat in the last row. Nobody could think what would happen thereafter. Wonder and fear struck all of us from tap to toe.

Sanjay turned impatient. His fist got hardened and he thumped on the desk. Pens, books and notes got scattered. He shouted at Saraswati, 'Yesterday you persuaded girls not to cast votes in my favour. Where are you from? How dare you so being a hosteller! I shall burn your face with acid. Even God won't be able to recognise you.'

He snatched Saraswati's veil even before anyone could know what happened and left the place. Yet the terrible moment didn't disappear from the classroom and the college campus. The college was closed for somedays in fear of further disturbance.

The college reopend. But none saw Saraswati - her eyes wavy, lips red, and her veil about to fall. It was known she was admitted in the college nearby her village.

Mango trees on the college campus were full of mango buds. Instead of hot and exciting arguments all wanted the answer to that question unanswered. Because the examination was drawing nigh.

It was doubtless we would forget Saraswati. Forgetting is natural. Nature has taught this. So without expressing any reaction I forgot her.

I never expected a strange scene had waited for me at Kamakhyanagar where I was transferred.

From Kamakhyanagar to Batgaon. Five kilometers away from that, there was a residential school. Our jeep halted under a sal tree there. A rainsoaked dawn. Drops of rain were trickling on earth. The earth was wet. That made the colour of the soil more red. Prayer was heard through silence.

The surroundings were filled with greenery.

I got off the jeep and entered the school. May be slabs of stone had life. A flower of yellow hue burst forth from them.

Saraswati was found standing in folded hands. Do the flower of love get scattered on soil and in heart? In fact, I was taken aback as I met her after so many days.

Her face had no trace of disappointment, or grief. But it betrayed an overwhelming emotion surging in her.

She chuckled. Her lips turned more red. In an unusal gesture she said, 'I read your stories. No more do thery dwell on rebellion. Love is their only theme. Do you think that is my only indentity? How many stories have you written about me? Would I be offering you soft touches of love experiences?'

Her words put me into shame even though I met her after so long. In fact, I didn't know that she was there. The fact is some presents are given away by our bank at different schools every year. This year a water filter was to be presented. My colleagues had rightly decided it to be given to a residential school.

There was life in the sal woods - Saraswati said. To think that any town in India could afford romantic esxperience, would be meaningless, after listening to this.

Sumanta and Ajay reached Kamakhyanagar after

fifteen days. Though aged, they looked quite vibrant. As if they were quite agog to compete between themselves to be intoxicated for any whim.

Just after a shower of rain the sky looked cloudy. We, three got into the jeep. The driver held the steering.

- Is county liquor(handia) available here? I shall drink. - asked Ajay.

Sumanta roared in laughter and said, 'O, do you want to drink *handia* and dance with adivasis? Listen, I have brought rum from Delhi. Drink as much as you like. You won't be inebriated at all. Simply you will experience swimming in the air.'

There stretched the woods of sal trees at two sides of the road. It started raining. Streams of rain water flowed from the jungle to the road. Red water. Kurei flowers scattered fragrance. With a log of wood overhead, an adivasi girl appeared from behind sal trees. Wet- her face, body and the clothes she had put on.

The rain united the sky, the sal jungle and the hill. Water filled the hillside. Water also ran along the serrated paddy fields. So was water in hearts.

The sky got cleared by the time we reached Kankadahad. The Guest House stood beside the dam. Arrangements had been made there. We had to climb steps. The sal trees cast their shadows. Ajay sat down there to quell exertion. Said he, 'In fact, life is here. Any despair of living disappears here. The bewitching Nature has filled here with enthusiasm. I had no such experience beforehand. In fear of wife, I have spent time.'

I apprehended he might say something more serious. But that didn't happen. Roaring laughter of young persons of a picnic party was heard at the dam site. Quite spontaneous, unstoppable.

For so many years, I have been busying myself to do my work alone . I didn't venture to do any other thing except getting imprisoned in the steel frame of bureacracy. Now also I am trying to continue in that cocon even after retirement. To this end, I have met our Chief Minister. After reaching here I feel everything was fruitless.

Sumanta's emotional ejaculation rang a note of surprise amid such surroundings.

Hot rice meat of fowl, *kankan* fry, salad of cucumber and tomato and curd were served on sal leaves.

After the meal, we spent time discussing politics and literature. The wind blew gently. We fell into a sleepy state.

When we woke up we perceived vast silence near the dam. Twittering of birds returning to their nests we heard.

- How far is Saraswati's school from here?' asked Sumanta. Ajay smiled a little and said, 'Well, do you plan to walk to that place all alone? Won't take me with you?'

Sumanta didn't reply. But stared at the sky, quite bemused.

I wiped my face and said, 'We will meet that on our return journey. But it's not possible to go there now. The driver is overdrunk, hence senseless. We have to wait till he regains consciousness.'

Gradually darkness crept into the hillside from the cleavage of leaves. On the full moon night moonbeams trickled from the sky. The dam shone brightly. Its water sparkled.

Sumanta and Ajay got down the steps. At last I too. The fragrance of wild kurei flowers was spreading everywhere faithfully. Such fragrance is not available so easily.

My concentration wavered along the stream of water . I asked, 'Hello! whose face is this? Sumant's or Ajay's?'

Ajay objected and said, 'Yours. Jayanta, it's your face. You have put on spectacles of thick lens, not we.'

His next experience brought about a reversal. Ajay was surprised and said, 'Whose bald head is that? Not a thread of hair is there. It shows old age.'

Sumanta appeared perturbed. He left the stream of water all at once, loitered along and across the dam in a state of restlessness. May be he could not arrive at a decision correctly. He approached me continuosly and asked, 'Is Saraswati as beautiful as before?'

Apparently I was waiting for such a moment. Sumanta was already uncontrolled by the fragrance of kureiflower. I said to him, 'Look, She is a *siddha yogini*. Time has been defeated by her.'

It seemed my mind so long restless became still in the water. I felt there was no more the necessary of the descent of that scene getting disturbed for many years to lead a life of fulfilment.

While returning Sumanta declined to turn the jeep towards the school near Batagaon. It appeared, his further meeting with Saraswati was insignificant.

A while later he said, ' I felt somewhat helpless after Sanjay had snatched the veil from Saraswati's bosom. Indeed I was dumbfounded. I had never imagined that man would be so helpless. Somebody in me awoke, emboldened me to fight. The state I have achieved today is due to that scene. To get rid of the fear of getting defeated anywhere.'

Quite stupefied, I looked. An incantation was heard from the sal jungle. Who did it - the sky, the earth or Saraswati?

The Song in a Fullmoon Night

Sanjay descended conventiently to the first floor after climbing fourteen stairs and encountered a scene, quite dramatic. Charulata emerged from the house. That was enough to stop him at the door. He turned passionless. His face got paled.

- Hello, Why enter the house this way? Haven't I cautioned you to keep shoes outside? You have never heeded. I am afraid you won't go by that. I cleaned every space just now. Then how did it get soiled?

All got lost - the blue sky, the wind blowing gently, the chirping of a hilarious bird. Very difficult to find these out again.

Charulata could easily catch,

Sanjay's silent agony.

Full of consolation, she asked him, 'Are you sick? This is Corona time. I told you to stroll in front of the house. Did you go to the river side? And what's in your house?'

Enlivened, Sanjay said in a low tone, 'Ah! I have forgotten to tell you - this flower sapling can sing; only in the fullmoon night. The seller told handing it over me. I forgot his name. He sells flower saplings behind the bank's boundary.'

That may be a stupefying moment which none ever experienced, I surmise.

So Charulata gazed at him for a while.

She thought it wise to remain silent.

- 'Plant it on a vacant space below. But keep it secret lest there should be a crowd on the fullmoon night. Consequently, the sapling couldn't sing amid confusion.' Sanjay spoke with more gravity that appeared mysterious.

Charulata asked him inquisitively if, while coming, he had broached this to any one.

Sanjay smiled. It expressed all mysterious experiences of life were in his hands, as it were. Like wings of the butterfly.' I can't remember.' he said.

Charulata was in a fix what more to ask but could realise Sanjay had a similar answer to all her questions. Like leaves falling in Spring. Sanjay used to be impervious to emotions dissimilar. While in service he never gave Charulata a chance to mark this so attentively. Naturally he remained busy always. However, after retirement he spent time, writing stories, planting flower saplings and gazing at the blue sky through window. Beside, he would feel unimaginable contentment and supreme silence.

But did it connote life's fulfilment and contentment?

Charulata would be surprised when she came across Sanjay's any interview published in newspapers. His words expressed he had no grief.

During his service period he failed to build a house. He had purchased a piece of land somewhere in a deserted place.

It has remained without a boundary till now. Sanjay would be careless even if someone possessed it illegally. Even he was attached to his paternal property in the village. Even the information that someone had encroached it didn't bother him.

- Why do you purchase so many flower saplings? Do

you remember we live in a rented house? You forget everything. How many times should I remind you of this? If you so like, give me the sapling. Let me plant it somewhere below. Would it bear flowers or sing songs only?

Charulata felt shaken while she expressed it. She felt a little excited about the incident that had happened a few years back. The fragrance of jasmine wafted gently by the zephyr. The window was open. Beyond it, twinkled bright stars. She looked at them througout the night like an unknown guest. She felt grateful towards Sanjay as if she got drowned in a sea of emotion. High tide she experienced throughout her body.

That was a mysterious moment drenched in unspeakable delight.

But where has that star gone? That extended emotional moment too was no more. Sometimes at midnight she would wake up and make a search for that star. But in vain. Even though she would wipe her face with the wet hem of her sari time and again, the sky and the star would not be seen. She would feel shrunk and confounded. None had ever remarked her as a beautiful daughter-in-law or that she appeared as golden.

Such experiences have startled and made her diffident again and again. Since the way of life is full of ironies and wonders, she has accompanied Sanjay all through. Never has she looked back. Even though relationship, whatsoever, appeared to be shadowy, she has allied herself not with her destiny but with Sanjay's destiny. That's why, her family now appears absorbing. She knows eventhough the moon on the fourteenthday disappears behind the mango tree, it would rise more beautifully the dayafter.

Life requires a home for its living. A home where all are content; its kitchen not having even a little soot; on its dining table are kept glasses full of water; there would be no hunger, no scarcity inside it, apparels arranged in almirahs; no dust on its reading table but piles of books, paper weight, pen; on its walls art of waves in the sea where float a handful of flowers of plenitude, faith and love. In the prayer room the deity would appear vibrant; prayer and chanting of mantras would be heard from here at dawn and dusk. One could not experience even a trace of darkness and solitude.

Of course, this inheres immeasurable void. Charulata feels it easily. Hence she cleans it and all furniture inside. Footprints, dust, envy and fear of the world can't cross the threshold.

Charulata descended on stairs, holding the flower plant sapling.

She heard sounds of foot and conversation in low tone. She crossed all this and approached the boundary wall and stood. The soil was soft; so was sand; a shower of rain rained last night. The wet soil was upturned; the tree with its green leaves stood straight. Raindrops fellon its leaves and roots.

The tree and its leaves looked ashen no more.

Charulata's lips trembled in glee. Her body got brightened. O, how easily one's mind and nature all around turn lively! While arranging her sari, she heard Suchitra's petrified tone, 'Where are you mother! O, father!'

Charulata was at a loss, failed to fathom what happened to Suchitra; one of her pair of chappals slipped off her foot; She got entangled in her sari. She was breathless to reach the threshold. The entire sky appeared bursting with lightning , thunder, swirling wind. It rained cats and dogs.

A moment of improbability. Features of the room turned diametrically opposite. Everything was enveloped with darkness and tears.

Suchitra was standing, her face sullen. The world of gaiety was transformed in a while.

Charulata failed to comprehend suddenly what actually had occurred. In her absense, a tornado of misery and imsfortune had blown pushing the door of her confidence and belief.

Sanjay had fallen flat on the floor. His breath very low. None could deny his breath might stop any time. Impossible to think it might stop anytime. Impossible to think how much she was capable to withstand such a situation. To strengthen her, Suchitra told, 'You just lift father with me. We will stretch him on the cot. Hope he would breathe conveniently.'

Then she halted at the doorstep. Sudden apprehension engulfed them. None ...

Time passed as tears trickled down. Charulata cursed herself. Why was she still alive to see such a scene? How did Sanjay fall down? May be he had sustained a major head injury. She caressed his brow and face. Had she been in the house, such accident might not have taken place.

'My legs slipped there and my chest...' Sanjay spoke faintly. The room reverberated with the sound of breathing almost suspended. Perhaps that is the only truth in the world.

Tears trickled down Charulata's cheeks, her face got wet with tears.

- 'What shall I do, if you become worried so much? I have called for the driver; he is coming. Get ready, we will go.' Perplexed, Suchitra said.

An uncontrollable tone of pathos burst out. Charulata asked, 'Where?'

Sobs gushed forth from heart, the cavity of grief . Suchitra's countenance turned pallid. She said, 'Nursing home. Can you repose faith in God any more? Only Nursing Home could turn the tide; not your prayer room.'

For the first time Charulata experienced the moment turning ruthless so accidentally.

She sprang up in unbound power as if she were beyond her control. Her mobile rang; a nervous tone from the other end was heard, 'Sister informed me over phone. How is father? Don't get lost. Buses are not plying. I shall hire a car, I may be late to reach there. Tell me the name of the nursing home where you are admitting him.'

They took twelve minutes to climb down those fourteen stairs. Roads petrified; barricades at each square; shops closed. Only at medicine shops were loitering some unhealthy faces; an ambulance was running blowing siren. The atmosphere was aghast as the shadow of corona had cast its shadow everywhere. Faces were hidden under masks, so was lost one's courage and identity. Wherefrom came the disease! Was it a disease or death-warrant?

They stopped the vehicle. As if flouting the government order and coming outside was an inexcusable offence! The order cautioned all to remain indoors so as to remain healthy. How could the vehicle be driven in contravention of this? The baton in the police hand could teach discipline. The policeman shouted, 'Don't you know everyone is prohibited to come outside at this crisis? How much could we explain it to you?'

Suchitra's hands folded in utter perplexity. She said, 'Father suffers from heart trouble. He feels it hard to breathe. So we are heading for a nursing home. Please let us...'

Palpitation of heart. Not a second to be late. The police said, 'Patient. Let him go.'

Suchitra felt troubled in multiple fears. She wiped

sweats on her father's brow. Sanjay's hands looked wet in spite of repeated wiping.

'Increase the speed. We must reach the Nursing Home as soon as possible.' - Suchitra shrilled.

It was not a moment to be or not to be. They must reach the Nursing Home on time. It has got all means to keep man alive; to repair the mechanism in his body. She was prepared to face the crisis. However, what was needed was to repose faith in respiration. But who can do that?

The vehicle turned right at the traffic stand. A few minutes later, they would be at the Nursing Home quite visible now. There would be doctors, stethescopes hanging from their necks. Oxygen cylinders must have been kept ready. Saline and a ventilator in ICU too. Suchitra had already consulted the Nursing Home.

The vehicle stopped. Closed was the gate. None dared to open it lest Corona Virus should enter the Nursing Home. So the gate and entrance to the Nursing Home as well was closed very gently the security man informed them.

Suchitra was nonplussed - where would she go? The patient and confidence solidified in her so long started melting. Tears welled up in her eyes, her mind fumed in rebellion. To be helpless in the middle of the road made her anxious. She said, 'Let's go to the government hospital.'

See, how the pain inside can make man so much invalid.

How much time it would take to reach the government hospital situated at a distance of five miles? All were speechless. Answer to such a question by anyone was of no a vail. But the most important thing was how soon they would reach there. While the entire world appeared immobile, the vehicle moved. There was a curve in front. So were rows of medicine shops; a *Kadamba* tree stood there too. The government hospital was to the left side. Their vehicle halted in front of the outdoor. Suchitra almost jumped off the vehicle.

She spoke emotionally, 'Please, help us a little; My father suffers from heart problem. Feels much pain in breathing. Who is the doctor to treat him? How can I meet him? He is in the vehicle. Let me know of the doctor and I shall immediately bring him there.'

They heard her incoherent words though, none appeared to turn sympathetic. Only a person at the counter said, 'First do Covid test; then we will start treatment. Otherwise we might be infected.' He uttered these in such a manner as though he were determined to free the world from Covid and were careful about every patient; he was more apathetic to anyone's voice terrified.

- 'Please listen to me. Father is not suffering from fever.

He was being treated in that Nursing Home, Alas! as it was closed   we faced all trouble. I supplicate you in folded hands, please call in the doctor, he will treat my further. My father' - Suchitra turned firm. While she folded her hands, her voice sounded a bit different. May be the person at the counter became conscious of his duty and said, 'Fill in a form there. The doctor is in his chamber. Take the patient in a wheel chair there.'

Suchitra appeared as swift as the wind. She rolled the wheel chair; opened the door of the vehicle, put Sanjay against her shoulder and made him seated straight easily. She was almost mad. Where was the doctor? In which chamber? She found a crowd all around her. An unhealthy atmosphere prevailed at the corridor. She saw nurses in white apron. She crossed all and could reach the bespectacled doctor. Sitting   aslant forward. She felt assured. She didn't think how much time they took to be there. No more to thinks of that... Now respiration would be set right; ill times would pass; The world would be smiles and smiles . Not an ordinary feat.

Yet Suchitra was getting overwhelmed with enxiety and perplexiety.

The stethescope in the doctor's hand moved and stopped on Sanjay's chest time and again. What was he doing? Sanjay was silent and immobile. Didn't respond when called. The attendant lifted Sanjaya from the wheelchair and laid him in bed.

After examinging, the doctor said slowly, 'He is dead.'

The world got shaken. Eyes closed. The floor shrunk down. No more tear in her eyes, Suchitra held the wheel chair. Who can shed tears with so much grief? In fact, she couldn't cry. Only stared at Sanjay's face. She couldn't believe how life departed so easily. She was no more eager to do anyother thing. She appeared to have been detained at a place. She had no effort or interest to go forward.

Her mobile rang. Who called her after all was over? Shuva, her younger brother spoke in a sullen voice, " Police did n't permit me to go. Because Bhubaneswar is under red zone. Please consult the doctor and admit him to a nursing home. Don't be worried, I am coming tomorrow. Things will be ok.'

- 'How can I explain to you father is no more. I failed to do anything for him.' Her tone became heavy, eyes got bedimmed. Everything appeared dark. Perhaps her head reeled. Suchitra inclined against the wall. She didn't know what more waited for her.

A deadbody in a stretcher was being carried outside. Suchitra dragged herself in the corridor. No more was she taken aback. She felt time had slipped off her hand somewhere so faithfully, it won't come back.

Nor would Sanjay call her as if he woke up from slumber.

A lot of papers to be signed in the midst of worthless moments.

Charulata - silent and unable to cry. As if her eyes had no tears.

- Is Shuva coming? - She asked

The question made her helpless. Irresistible became her tears. Tears and sobs got amalgamated with irrepressible grief. Now she felt pain and only pain and was anxious illimitably to tide over such grief. How ever, she lost herself in the midst of impenetrable darkness and solitude.

She brushed her cheecks with her hands and said, 'Let's take the deadbody home.'

A hard time indeed. The river of faith and stream of confidence and courage would get dried wherever you set foot. Nobody came forward to extend help in such weal and woe. They found the gate locked when they reached home. They heard her voice. But none unlocked the gate.

A grief still reigned. Her conviction, courage, faith, prayer got shadowy.

Suchitra could know the gate would not be opened. It was the house owner's well- thought-out conspiracy. Since they had returned from hospital, he was afraid, Corona virus would infect. Who would listen to her? May be, fear of death can make all unconscionable. Consequently, time would turn timid.

What bird chirped in a branch of the tree? Suchitra couldn't know it in nocturnal darkness.

- 'How far is the burial ground?' She asked very gently.

The vehicle ran forward.

Quite an unknown road. Tall trees at its two sides.

Incomprehensible darkness and incredible solitary atmosphere. Three to four ill-clad, emaciated persons were busy. Pungent smells of burning corpses suffocated them. Hopeless darkness enveloped the cabin. She could see the visage of the goddess.

A police van horned and stopped there. Somebody in khaki uniform got down, his eyes sparkling. In a heavy tone he asked, 'What's your problem?'

It was time to be afraid. Suchitra said, "We are waiting. My brother is coming."

- How much time would he take to arrive here?

Suchitra felt exhausetd. In a trembling voice she said, 'Five to six hours.'

- Do you know what hours of night now? And you will wait for five to six more hours at the burial ground! Who are with you?

Suchitra's throat got dried. She said, 'Mother.'

The police officer was startled; he stared at her. In a dissuading tone he told, 'Look. There is lock down throughout the country. Nobody moves an inch. Don't you feel afraid? Don't wait any more. It's ten. Perform cremation and go back home.'

Suchitra caught the meaning of what she heard. She had no answer for this except drops of tears.

Everything was arranged for cremation. Flower, parched paddy, towel, earthen pot, match box, earthen lamp, incense sticks, dry wood. Fire burned in the hearth. Rice was boiled in an earthen pot. When Suchitra offered the half-boiled rice to the deadbody's face, she felt that was not her father's. It was so dark, so terrible!

The face was not at all the face of a story loving person.

She lit the pyre and returned to the vehicle without looking back. She was speechless as everything was getting finished in the raging flame, burning wood and envelping smoke.

While returning Charulata said, 'It is not yet dawn.'

More solitude, more void encircled her. The sky was covered with doubtful darkness. It was impossible to find out the stars.

Tears in Charulata's eyes appeared starlike. Suchitra gazed at such brilliant wonder.

The story ends here. But can it be so this way!

A very unimaginable scene was seen after two months. Charulata received from a courier, a book recently published and sent by some publisher at Delhi. Pensive, she sat near a window, saw a tree that had spread its branches, leaves, etc. The gentle wind stirred in her a searching mood. The book was on the table.

Complete silence in the house. Suchitra had a streak of surprise on her face.

Jutst then Sanjay's colleague Srikanta entered like a well-acquainted person. He used to accompany Sanjay in his morning walk. He sat in the sofa and without any introduction he straight way handed a pass book to her.

- 'He had given me the pass book to update it. May be he forgot to bring it back. I was also unable to come in fear of Corona. So the pass book was with me.' As he saw the book on the table, he was surprised and asked, 'Is his new book published after his departure?'

He held the book, opened its pages, smiled but soon his face looked miserable and anxious.

- He has dedicated the book to Sunanda. Indeed he was a story-oriented person who looked at clouds. Could comprehend birds chirping. Do you know, whenever he would sit on the river's embankment, some bird would come and sit in his lap. They would peck at the rice in his hand to devour. Undoubtedly the name of one of those birds was Sunanda. He used to call her by this name and the bird would reply chirping. Nobody could comprehend what the bird said."

Bemused, Charulata looked at Suchitra. How come the mind of a story teller was so incomprehensible! Could she express the perplexing mental conflict she had suffered for three to four days?

Srikanta thought what more to speak out. He sipped coffee and said, 'A simple person. Believed everybody. He never forgot anything though he simulated forgetting. Otherwise, how could he spin yarn so much?'

He paused and sipped coffee again. Then said, 'Always he would purchase plants of various flowers. He used to say he had a piece of land where he would build a house and plant flower plants there. Once a plant seller showed him a flower plant and told him that it could sing in a full moon night. Alas! Sanjay was obsessed with stories. How could he judge - hence he had purchased that - for one thousand rupees.'

A mysterious solitude spread. Yet nobody was able to know that Sanjay was singing on the river bank in that fullmoon night. His face and heart were resplendent with the peculiar effulgence of the star.

The Golden Sunari Flower

The star-spangled sky. Fragrance of jasmine flowers all around. Unimaginable darkness there. The sound of a gate opened was heard amid that murkiness. The shrunk environment was not hospitable to any entrance into the school.

Someone, a lantern in hand, cautioned very accidentally. The lantern glass was dark as it had been kept burning for a longtime.

The young Alok Mohanty, my second polling officer who followed me, said, 'Sir, please take steps cautiously and follow me. Current has been off before an hour. I have been waiting here. The Headmaster went to his house. He gave me responsibility.'

'We were late because of receiving of EVM and documents necessary for elections. Our vehicle also ran out of order on the way manytimes. Also the driver halted almost half an hour to take meal.'

The man was not prepared for such an answer. Confusion was manifest in his demeanour He failed to present an exact account of how much time he had waited for us. He unlocked the door hastily, pushed it dispassionately. The room was slightly lighted inside. A duree had been spread on the floor; there were five to six tables beside the wall, an earthen water pot and a glass. Some chairs waited for that uncertain moment.

All on a sudden the room was lighted as current came. May be they should not be irritated any more. The man folded his hands, took leave of me in such a manner that I thought I won't meet him again.

Alok knew it was a different environment, a difficult situation. Yet time was scheduled. He drew out of the trunk some forms, files, chits of red and white colours and a lantern operated by battery. He switched it on. The room became bright, clear because the letters and sleepy faces were more visible. We were tired. There was complete silence.

Alok said in a feeble and fumbling tone, 'I would have gone to see the girl. Her house is eight to ten kilometres away from our village. Of course, I have seen her casually once or twice when she was getting down the bus.'

His lively words, full of love, seemed to be a love letter. He did not know what more to add to that letter. He asked me. Alas! I had no proper answer to that. Though I knew the art of living, I had no knowledge of the art of loving.

Like the tune of Akshya Mohanty's song the slow wind touched my mind. I was practising singing in childhood. I would purchase from the bazar a song in Hindi and sing loudly. That, too, without proper note. It would irritate mother and she didn't forget to inform it to father. Yet they were not serious about it. They were much concerned about my elder sister's marriage. After graduation, she was simply spending time at home. She was averse to enjoying TV always. Rather she was interested in witnessing the kind of sarees the girls adorned themselves with when getting married.

I fared miserably in the Test Examination. Father felt let down. He admitted me to a school at Gobindapur not far from Dhenkanal. It was beside a hillock. I stayed in the boarding house adjacent to the school. In its front were a well and a small garden. Manorama, Ramakrushna sir's daughter, used to draw water from the well and water flower plants. Her responsibility it was. Slim and fair though, she was smarter. Her two braids of hair hanging on her breast betrayed all possibilites. She used to join two clips at the braid's tail that appeared like wings of the butterfly .

Buds would patiently await the whole day. Manorama would touch and kiss them in the afternoon. Her touch would blosssom flowers and the wind would be fragrant. A careless shadow would appear on the otherside of the window; winkless indeed. But who can wink to lose such a scene! Even a one-eyed boy used to struggle to enjoy himself of the scene for a long time. Though he knew not what he saw; He saw green grass; mud, worms in the garden and got overwhelmed. Yet he contemplated that the world was blessed with a more beautiful scene. Perhaps he had not seen a more beautiful damsel.

Still I remember how some books were stolen. Ramakrushna Sir felt dismayed. But who had stolen? Each student suspected the other. Everyone's trunk was searched. It was a heart-rending moment . Some books were found in the trunk of a one-eyed boy. A distresssing scene spread - how could the boy be so ungrateful! Speechless, Ramakrushna Sir cast a side glance and went inside the house.

God knows why I felt sympathetic towards that boy who was going to sit for the matirculation examination with me. He was poor and fatherless. His mother had brought him to Ramkrushna Sir's care. She had hoped he would read, be honourable, and get employed. But he read novels. For somedays, he kept silent though he hummed indistinctly while watering flower plants. But he was sure nothing was useless. Like plenitude, love is essential and meaningful in life. At times he would wipe tears from his eyes. So that his ugly face would look more faded.

I knew the situation would turn anxiety-ridden. That also turned out. Manorama wiped his tears and the scene made me dumbfounded. It was quite impossible to put up with this. I hit upon a plan which my village classmates accepted without any if and but. Manorama was given charge to make Ramkrushna Sir agree to our proposal. He too did not refuse. Saptasajya was not that far off. One could return in the evening if one went there in the morning. Sir also thought his students would be free from drudgery of rigorous study if they went there for some time.

We rode bicycles - laughing uproariously. As if, it were our campaign to conquer a fort! I carried that boy on my cycle carrier. A cap on head, Manorama paddled her own bicycle. She hang a bag in her cycle handle. Our speed made passers-by move aside. The scared birds flapped their wings in the sky. The crows got frightened. . The wind blew gently in the mango groves. The golden oriole sang melodiously. Scarves flew with gaiety galore.

A fountain was murmuring. Shoals of golden fish were swimming in water. The high mountain range led us onward. We reached Saptasajya at a stretch. As Manorama washed her face with the fountain water, she looked more captivating. Our bicycles stood against the trunk of a mango tree. All of us drew edibles out of our bags - biscuits, mixture, sweets, etc. We ate the cake Manorama's mother had sent. Then we drank the clean fountain water. We bacame very happy.

I saw Manorama smiling and that made her more magnetic. I looked at her face enxiously.

She said, 'Will you listen if I sing a song?'

Who can deny such an offer in such an environment? Manorama drew out a song note from her bag. It contained a lot of songs. We heard the cooing of a cuckoo at a distance. From this thick foliage of mango trees. I became curious and looked around to ascertain from which tree the sound came. At last my attention got fixed on a vehicle. None was found inside. Only a camera was on a seat. Would it look nice if a photograph was snapped?

Now Manorama sang. Who can lose such a moment? Only I was loving Manorama. Cautiously I caught the camera in my hand and came to the mango tree. The boy who had accompanied us listened to the song.

I clicked the camera. Lo, Manorama's photograph emerged from it incredibly! I held it in my hand and pushed it into my pocket instantly. Then I handed over the camera to the boy. He couldn't understand what happened. Shouts of joy started before one could perceive what happened.

All of us were on our bicycles. It was not necessary for us to paddle. We climbed down speedily. At the foot of the hill, there was a rose garden. Our bicycles rolled onward along that zigzag way raising reddish dust. After a while we found the vehicle not running behind us. We needed rest and drank water.

- What's that? Why did you commit theft? asked Manorama dispassionately.

The boy appeared miserable. He pulled out something from his bag and showed us. None could recognise it. The boy was almost mute. Everyone looked at me.

- Camera; we will take our group photograph after we reached our hostel. So that we could remember one another. God knows who will be where after our examination! But the photograph will make us remember.

But the matter didn't appear relevant. However, was it possible to accept this in such circumstances?

- Those should be returned - said Manorama. But nobody knew how to return.

Moments that followed were not at all pleasant. Yet there was much shout and much paddling.

Ramkrushna Sir was confused. He came out of his room as he heard shouts.

At the moment one Bengali gentleman shouted from the vehicle and explained in a low voice that these boys had stolen his camera.

Ramkrishna Sir was beside himself with anger.

- Who has stolen? Where is the camera? he snarled.

The camera was seen in that boy's hand. It appeared to be costly. It was a terrible moment. The boy's face looked confounded. His sobbing trembled everywhere. It was seen after sometime that a stick broken had fallen on the ground.

After two months, I returned to Dhenknal.

Our Board Examination began. Our examination centre was Joranda. I plied to the centre by bus everyday, returned to Cutttack after the examination . Thereafter there was no scope to know about Manorama. Even today I am ignorant of her whereabouts.

I could perceive by Alok's words that I had not seen Manorama clearly. I should have seen her smile and captivating look. However, time past never returns. No more would Manorama appear before me confidently. I felt terribly miserable at that time.

The night passed with ill thoughts and sheer helplessness.

Clear and calm was the dawn.

The table inside the room was well arranged . On it was the EVM machine - one for Parliament election and another for Assembly. Two sheets of paper on which 'ENTRANCE' and 'EXIT' had been written had been pasted on the door. The inkpot was in front of Alok. He was in charge of marking a voter's finger with ink.

Time slid. After some habitual talks we conducted mock polling in presence of polling agents. I felt assured, everything was all right. My worries evaporated. I looked all around. It was Spring. A sunari flower plant laden with flowers stood at the other side of the window. Its golden petals were being scattered in the sky, as it were.

The polling started at 7AM. A turbaned, aged person, sporting a thick moustache, entered with his voter indentity card in hand. The first polling officer felt embarrassed to locate his serial number. However, a while later he found the person's identity card matched his name. No problem then. Alok inked the voter's nail. The voter was given a chit. The EVM produced a sound thereafter.

The sense of fear and uncertainty disappeared. Because of a smile. Voters, one after another, cast their votes and left through the exit. But a shout was created by the crowd, on the other side of the door. Voters on the school campus were jubilant and avid while political persons remained busy applying their unbelievable strategy. The police were alert all through. Everything appeared going on smoothly. Candidates' future was being imprisoned in the ballot box.

The wind swayed boughs of the sunari tree. It nursed no expectations. Simply it wished to exhibit its beauty. To me, it appeared not the bough of the sunari tree but Manorams's song flying in my mind's firmament.

- What do you look at? Some fake voting has already occurred. What farce is going on here?

I felt a strong push on my shoulder. I was about to

fall. I could n't know to which political party the person standing in my front, belonged. Immediately he left the room like a storm. The police were unable to restrain him.

Another unimaginable scene followed. An elderly lady, after casting her vote, stood in my front, caressed my shoulder and looked at me so passionately that none before had done so. I felt a wave of tremulation. As if, I would be overwhelmed! And fly skyhigh in the shower of affinity.

Along with her I came outside. Stood at the shade of the sunari tree and saw Manorama had held the elderly lady's hand.

- I stay here, teaching children. My father expired two years back. My mother lives withme. Well, what about you? - she said.

Manorama was in myfront, clad in a saree of light blue colour. No more did her braid hung on her breast or fly in the sky. Her dishevelled hair, her exposed neck, her cheeks, lips - in all, her symmetrical physique was bewitching.

- What is that boy doing now? She queried after a while. I felt embarrassed and asked, 'Who?'

With a chuckle she said, 'Well, that boy in whose trunk a novel was found and his face appeard sobbing.'

- I don't know his whereabouts.

Heaving a deep sigh, Manorama said, 'I was sure you had some information about him. May be you have met him. Do you know, he possessed a beautiful world in his painful mind. May be, therefore he was able t embrace reality. He knew sorrows contained happiness and love. When he left the hostel, he presented me a book.'

Startled I asked, 'What type of book?'

- A poetry book.

My overwhelming joy and absorption vanished. Full

of despair and dejection I returned to the polling booth. It was not at all an ordinary matter. Ranjan was my competitor, I admitted.

The polling was over just at four. The EVM was sealed. The polling agent took leave. We arranged the ballot papers, voter list, forms and necessary documents.

I felt overwhelmed. The entire surroundings looked terrible and deformed when the CRPF shouted. The vehicle would come. We have to return by another route. There was news that the Moists had targeted us. As it was night we got more petrified. We felt wounded, fatigued and we switched off our mobile phones. We didn't know how long we walked. The police force encircled us in that night. I couldn't broach that I had stolen the book and put it in Ranjan Rout's trunk.

I failed to visualise Ranjan's face though I thought about him in my depressed mind. Like golden fish playing in a fountain water, the colour of the sunari flower glistened. My be, I was able to walk all night, being wet with that colour. Can it be called love? If you meet Manorama, tell her I, not Ranjan Rout, love her. I am waiting to cover the remaining distance of life with her.

The Mantra

A wonderful star in the clean, star-studded sky. Its bright face appears on the other side of the window after light is out. It looks like a jasmine flower . However, Sujata is no more interested to look at that face. She feels it is her duty to enjoy a sound sleep so much. She is unconcerned about any other role she has to play or do more work.

After marriage she has tried as far as possible to make her conjugal life consummate. She desires to make her house look more beautiful than the world. Jayanta's happiness is her delight. That's why, the colour of the curtain is red embroidered with sparkling flower and green leaves. But the colour is anathema to her. She likes green colour. It touches one's mind and heart like waves of the sea. She neither expressed her preference nor objected least when the curtain was purchased. The sky and the star vanished behind the thick curtain. She looks at her hesitating face in the mirror of darkness after light is out. Can one see one's face in such a mirror? What is seen - grief or love?

She is getting shrunk day by day because of uncertainty and perplexity. Who could she speak to about this? It has not been easy for her to spend a year this way. She has been struggling with herself. Getting defeated too. After defeat, she appears like a naive girl. She never thinks she occupies a significant place in the family. The home is furnished with costly furniture purchased as per Jayanta's choice and preference.- the sofa set, dining table, painting, and even fish in the aquarium. She wished to place here two fish of mixed colours - blue and golden. While they moved their tails, water in the aquarium would be scattered creating the illusion of waves in the sea. But Jayanta vetoed. On the otherhand, the shopkeeper packed seven to eight fish in a polythene packet. Sujata kept mum. My be she did not know how to protest or was ablivious of protest after marriage. In the meantime she was not aware that she had lost her emotional being altogether. She feels perplexed.

Now she experiences such moments. Even then she arranges bedsheet, pillow covers, small towels; hangs shirt, pant and punjabi in hangers. She fails to return to herself in spite of so much confusion. So she says to her mother inattentively, ' I don't feel the house as home. In spite of my cleaning it there ramins soot somewhere.'

Her mother keeps mum. After a little while she says gently, 'You will see the home will be very much yours. Jayanta is good. He may have neglected you as he is busy working. I know your mother-in-law is very affectionate.'

Sujata fails to comprehend why her mother's consolation is full of darkness and solitude. Mother is now alone after father's departure. May be she is shaky now. No possibility of her becoming strong again. This is not an ordinary matter. As if she sailed by a broken boat that allowed all water from all sea entering it. She knows it will drown in unfathomable water. None would extend a hand to save her.

Now she is in the vortex of adversity. She may drown any moment. None would extent their hand and help her come out.

Her mobile phone rang at this moment of conflicts

and helplessness. Sujata was sure Jayanta was calling. He would inform in a low voice "I shall be returning from the office. Don't wait for me.'

After such casual and undependable talk he would swith off his mobile. Sujata is sure Jayanta would spend time in a hotel not in the office. Dead drunk, he would return at night.

The mobile went on ringing . But she was irritated and callous to such ringing. Does much casual talk hold any meaning ? Would the heaven fall if he returnd late? Would her domestic life be ruined? Every day she used to arrange bedsheets, dresses herself with utmost care. Perhaps the world had preserved immense wealth for her just as layers of ornaments are placed in a jewellery shop. She would muster no courage to enter the shop and see any ornament there. How much do such ornaments cost?

As the mobile rang again she was compelled to switch it on. Mother asked, 'What's the matter? Why do you switch on your mobile so late?' Jayanta returned?

Helpless, Sujata asked, 'Mother, please tell me why does a jewellery shop keep ornament? I don't want to buy merely a necklace, but all ornament. O, yes, all ornament.'

It was indeed a dramatic moment. Sujata's words startled her mother at the other end.

She said, 'You are possessed! Otherwise how can you say this?'

Sujata didn't know whether to cry or laugh. Her mother-in-law was in the next room. The middle class inhibition caught hold of her being. The being that was denied even a bit of dream.

She laughed and said, 'Tell me what I should do. Because of power cut it is dark all round. I sought a little happiness in that darkness.'

Did mother feel how intimate the enjoyment of happinsess was?

She cried only. She has been crying more and more after fathers demise. At times, she would burst into tears without any rhyme and reason. It would flood the entire world, as it were. Mother's tear-soaked face would glisten in darkness.'

Gentle wind entered through the aperture of thick curtain.

After a while Sujata asked, 'How are you?'

Its answer was simple but for her mother it's much difficult. She was incredibly optimistic. So she said, ' Let us go to Ganeshkhole tomorrow. I had accompanied your father when he was alive. A sage stays there. He had predicted your marriage.'

This dramatic revelation startled Sujata - was it true? Can any one predict? It's foolishness to believe in this. God knew why after sometime she turned anxious. Her face exuded signs of surprise.

- When are you arriving here?

The interrogation shook the environment. The room got lighted. Like a phantom the prolonged darkness disappeared. In fact, does not one beg for someone's compassion or kindness ? After post graduation she was interested to sit for competitive examination to get a service. Mother said 'no' though father did not agree to that. However, his opinion did n't prevail and he decided to give Sujata in marriage. None understood Sujata's tenor of protest. They thought the proposal was appreciable . They became conscious of their responsibility.

Sujata's father passed away a month after her marriage, though he was not diseased. While delivering a speech on stage, he fell down like a tree felled. It was in vain to be worried for him. By the time they reached hospital, he was suffering from cardiac arrest. The doctor declared him dead instantly. Sheets of paper remained disarranged on the table. Perhaps mother had no courage to arrange them. She was confident father would return and resume writing his incomplete stroy as usual.

In reality, what was father writing? With whom was he conversing till dead of the night? It was totally meaningless to ask him if he met someone at that time.

Mother said - he used to converse with the charaters of the story and portray their trials and tribulations. Otherwise, how could he have known their stream of consciousness? Father used to say only a dear friend could mark how the stream of fear got wet in rain.

But how is it Jayanta fails to read her mind? How can she explain to him that she wants to enjoy a little bit of her individuality? She prays to God to have some liberty? So she never turns ungrateful to Him even if she is inflicted by so many problems.

She asked again, 'Mother, when are you coming? Please request my mother in law that I shall accompany you.' In the midst of so much comedy and emotion, the shadow of fear and anxiety spread. She didn't want it to be unfulfilled for any reason. She will enjoy some freedom from domestic burden if she was allowed to wander outside.

Mother arrived in a winter morning. She had wrapped a shawl on her body. She appeared slightly sickly. Though they lived in the same town she had seen her about two or three months back. My be mother was between hope and hopelessness which tortured her mentally.

A long pitch road ran from Bhubaneswar to Dhenkanal. Shady mango trees were beside it. The road from Dhenkanal to Joranda presented a scene of ripe corn field, bathed in fog. It was intense cold in December. Mother clasped her shawl. From Joranda an uneven road ran to Ganeshkhol blessing all with an intimate touch. The woods were full of greenery. Birds chirped. Nature appeared contented and stunningly charming. The clean small temple of Lord Ganesh stood there. Mother bowed to the deity and muttered something reverently; some white and yellow flowers scattered on the floor. That was enough to fill the devotee's mind with faith. The scene of the bel-leaves and the presence of Lord Shiva's image filled Sujata's mind with joy. What would she pray - for happiness or peace?

Her attention was drawn to a youngman while she wiped the sacred water of the deity's feet from her lips. Soft sunshines, full of promise, had scattered on the floor made of stones. Sujata felt wet in the wintry wind. Full of stunning wonders, she looked at the youngman. Unambiguous light of gratitude and probability returned to her, she felt. Sanjaya, tall, strong, not so fine in colour, stood in her front. After three to four years. He was champion in college sports.

- 'You are here!' she asked.

Very gravely Sanjay replied, 'My home is at Dhenkanal. I was on holidays here. So I came to this place. But why you...' Sanjay couldn't complete. May be he wanted to say something more but lost way. But not he, rather Sujata. Words stumbled in her throat.

She asked - Do you remember me, Sanjay?

- O, Yes. How do you think I could forget? Those things were not unreal for us. Surely there was some reality in that love too. Hope you understand what I say.

So much light in a winter morning. Not necessary. Sujata could hide her face if she got a little darkness somewhere.

Sanjay said in a comparatively low voice, 'I am at Pune now, drawing handsome salary. The company has provided me a flat and a car. A lawn and garden in front of the flat. Children gather and shout loudly in afternoons. I didn't know how you are. But my flat, filled with darkness, waits for me, till I return. None other than I is there.'

He uttered these words in such a way that expressed everything had been haywire. Darkness and hopelessness all around her, Sujata was spending life that way, in a flat at Bhubaneswar. She had everything but nothing. As if she lived in an immobile environment!

From his pocket Sanjay drew out his visiting card, handed it over to Sujata and said, 'Here is my address and mobile number. You can talk to me, may visit me if you so like.'

Sujata felt bewildered as if she had lost something somewhere.

The winter wind appeared more conducive. Sujata drew her saree on her bosom. It would have been better if she had brought her shawl. So that the neck and exposed back would have remained unexposed in the soft sunshine.

Like a floating leaf, Sanjay left waving his hand. After his departure Sujata stood in the morning sunshine for sometime. The bird's chirping, floating from boughs of the mango tree was sweet which she could not grasp easily. Perhaps love's language is incomprehensible like this. Mother approached her from the opposite direction, She asked, 'What are you doing here? I think you were talking with someone. It's your bad habit to talk with anyone shamelessly wherever you go.'

Sujata was not prepared to listen to this. So her eye lids became moist. Mother was responssible for the misfortune she had been suffering from. Otherwise she would not have come here so early in the morning and stood on the temple campus. She would return. That house, full of soots, would be her heaven.

She followed her mother very cautiously. The driver waiting under the mango tree opened the door. Mother sat in the car and arranged her saree.

- Won't you meet the sage? Sujata asked. Mother chuckled. She gave Sujata a piece of paper and said, 'Well. He had some work to do. So he went away. Why should he wait for you? I told him everything. He heard it attentively. He has written a mantra for the well-being of your conjugal life. If you chant it with all purity, your life will be filled with all types of happiness.'

Perhaps, while arranging papers, mother had read the incomplete story written by father that lay on the table.She believed father would complete the story after returning. That has kept her alive. That's why she takes her mother's words to be stories. She turns quizzical if truly the mantra of four to five words has power to make her conjugal life happy. Whether it would make her every moment painless, if she read it! Only Jayanta could see the tears trickling from her eyes and getting drenched in rain. Who should she ask - mother or the sage?

Silence reigned inside the car. Sujata had no sign of delight or wonder in her mind. It appeared she was in quest of finding ways to exist in that silence. For the first time, she discovered she was beyond herself. Rather she had a piece of paper in her hand. The paper contained a mantra. She kept on looking outside for a longtime.

An unknown bird in the blue sky flew towards the horizon. Neither had it known her nor had she known it. Yet, it had identiy. But why has she been living this way?

She was surprised and thought such questioning was not irrelevant. How could she forget she was the artist of her own life? How foolish she was because she had surrendered her brush to others!

After seven to eight days. An incredible occurrence took place. Jayant dashed against a sofa and escaped a fall fortunately. Still the hang over was there. What should he do? Where should he go? Sujata's letter lay on the teapoy. Sanjaya's visiting card as well as mother's paper on which the mantra was written was on the floor. Only it needed pious incantation.

Jayanta's voice became tremulous. He experienced slight heart burning. Quite helpless, he said to mother, 'Without talking to me, Sujata has fled to Delhi. She will research there. In her letter she has requested me to forget her. Rubbish! can anyone do like this? I didn't know she would be such crazy.'

No more could he say. He fell down like hailstone falling from the sky.

Nobody knew why mother chuckled. She closed her eyes and felt the incomplete story was complete after many days.

Her Sighs

Indeed, it was an incredible scene in the room. Nobody could comprehend what mother said. But the scene indicated the room was suffocated because of an illness in the world. No possibility of recovery. Mother's face turned pale day by day. It was so pale even she couldn't recognise it. And she won't be able to admit she had an individual indentity of her own. At times her feeble voice indicated she was alive. She would open her lips only when some liquid food was given. Her tongue looked small near her lips. Not to speak but to get wet a little with some drops of water. She was thirsty which she contained in herself with endless pain.

What and how could she speak? She had surely forgotten the rudiments of language. But she batted her eye lids a little; it indicated she wanted to speak something or she was in search of something. But what was that? The Gita had been kept near her pillow; it contained sermons about the art of living. But those were of no avail now. Deities had been installed in the adjacent room. Their visages looked bright. Some of them were clad in yellow cloth while others in blue cloth. Yet all of them were unconcerned. Something came to pass which should not happen, as it were.

The deity 'Anthua Gopal' had been brought from Brindaban;

father had brought her Jagannath from Puri. His face was pitch dark. It looked always in a gesture of assuring security. Mother became alone after father's death. Because she had no anxiety any more. She was oblivious of time, as it were. She would talk in the prayer room. But with whom for so long? At times, her buzzing halted . Grief and dejection remained inside the room.Time remained stagnanat in the prayer room, as it were. We were unable to feel her presence in the room. Perhaps she held a monologue with herself and looked at the deity and herself. At times every individual likes such soliloguy. That's the way God's benediction is sought. None except God had time to talk with mother. Father used to say during their sixty year old life, only mother heard their unending tales of life. She would nod her in between and get startled as her daughter in law and grandson and granddaughter were present in the same room.

Mother well understood perhaps relationship bacame loose when children grew up. That's why it was natural she was being gradually neglected by them. While one of them would spend moretime in college, the other would be busy enjoying cartoons. As each got ways to get himself or herself in his/her world, she was unheeded. She became unable to preserve some memories of father. She appeared somewhat indifferent when father's shoes were thrown into a heap of dirts. She couldn't cry too. May be since long tears had dried up in her eyes. But this much was perceived that she had lost herself by losing everything.

The happening was also similarly pathetic. She had no courage to raise a voice of protest. When my elder brother arranged the cot in father's room for himself, she remained immobile at the otherside of the door leaning against the wall. The wall was her only support. Otherwise how could she put up with such a deep grief? May be that was the photograh of their nuptial ceremony. Elder brother pulled it out of the wall and said, 'You don't need such a large room. You will put up in the room adjacent to the prayer room where I shall hang this photograph. You could see father.'

Mother realised. So do all mothers when their offspring growup. In fact she had no necessity of occupying such a large room. Everything appeared small when father was alive. In spite of large space, space was insufficient to put books. They ramained disarranged even though arranged time and again. May be they had hand and legs; they were moving inside the house. Talking with each other too. A table made of Indian Kino tree was there. A chair stood behind it. The open window faced east. Father used to sit there. He would appear very smart in morning sunshine. The rattling sound produced by the wood pecker would be heard at a distance. The fragrance of mango bud or at times of champak flowers spread all round. Mother would never enter the room when she found father writing. She would also caution me not to enter.

What was father writing? He used to give life to words on sheets of paper. But I had not understood this at that time. Because only the golden pen kept on the table drew my attention. It looked amazingly beautiful in sunshine. After father's departure, now the pen adorns my brother's shirt pocket. However, it does not look nice there at all. Yet he has kept it there. He also imitates father's way of walking. But mother very well recognises from his footsteps that those are not father's. Brother enters the room which is no more hers. The well-arranged books have lost their familar places also. A lantern, flat TV and some Kalion dolls have occupied that place. One would find mementos, certificates of appreciation no more. These have been lost in heaps of dust. Somehow I could save a few certificates of appreciation while those were being sold alongwith waste papers and have preserved.

Who remembers whom? Perhaps all get lost in the limbo of oblivion this way. Mother will not be there after somedays. We would forget her identity. How long could we remember her? We also could't remember father.

Father had no trouble. He had been to attend a literary meeting; suffered from cardiac pain while he was delivering speech. Felt terribly suffocated. On way to hospital, he passed away. None could holdback the air though many of his friends were present. It was incomprehensive how he breathed his last. The deadbody was brought home. Mother cried for the last time. Father could not listen to her cries any more. Perhaps she needed a little consolation, a little assurance too. Father would rise and say, 'Don't cry even though I am absent, I am present in this house. In books, in the character I have created.'

Circumstances changed. Mother bacame alone. She colud not be careful about herself. Because of so many disadvantages, her mind got shattered. She could not withstand father's, bereavement. Broken she became inside. No sobbing, no language was able to express it. One day, she slipped in the bathroom; her spinal cord was fractured. Acute pain spread througout her body. She was admitted to a nursing home. After twenty days we brought back her home. We believed in the doctor's assurance she would be able to walk. But that was not to be. The possibilities of her broken bones getting joined waned by dagrees. Then she suffered from another stroke that paralysed half her body, and turned her face and lips crooked.

How long could she survive in such a body? We

lost patience. Relatives also stopped visiting her. Annoyed, elder brother said, 'How long would we be troubled?'

Death is normal. So it was seen when the day broke mother lay dead on the cot. May be elder brother would be glad by getting such news. He would no more arrange her upper cloth. Because her world was different and contracted. Not at all...

Who else could have listened!

In such circumstances, sister Nilu sat beside her and tried to understand her words. Sister in law called her to go to the other room. But she has been sitting beside mother since her arrival.

She suffered from heart stroke before seven or eight days back. Thereafter this has been her condition. She was all right-before, able to speak, recognise people. In fact, it's a very difficult task to recognise man. It is not a wonder to recognise at the last moment of life? For her now they are unkown members of family with whom she was attached throughout her life. Then how she can recognise sister Nilam?

- You could have informed me earlier that mother was serious. So that I could have come. Now I lost an opportunity of not suffering from sorrows due to my inability to talking with her.

What elsle could she have experienced? Tears trickled down her cheeks and her lips got wet. She sobbed so much which expressed her mental agony. Sister in law felt her grief and helplessness and said, 'Please, don't cry before mother. Though unable to speak, she is able to understand whatever is done. She would be much aggrieved.'

A sense of remorse grew more and more in sister Nilu's mind. She cast a pathetic glance at mother and left with sister in law. At the dining table she said, 'I know you didn't inform me deliberately.'

Sister in law remained silent and busy cutting vegetables. Gradually sister Nilu's sobbing stopped. Perhaps she thought what to speak next. Water was boiling on the gas oven. Sister in law stopped cutting vegetables and added tea dust to the boiling water and milk then.

There came a moment of sympathy to the room. Perhaps the two tried to understand each other. Both were overpowered by grief. Drops of tears fell on the floor and drew them to a petrified world that contained only unconditional darkness.

- I don't like anything. I am so scared due to mother's illness that I can't remember anything. Unable to inform anybody. In fact, I forgot to inform you. You know what your brother is, he has no time. So busy that he leaves home at 9AM and returns in night. So saying, she handed over a cup of tea to sister Nilu.

She tried to create an idea about all this in such a manner that it appeared she was exclusively responsible for everything.

She placed some biscuits in the plate. Some flowers of affinity got scattered, as it were. Sister Nilu could't know the colour of that flower. She held the cup of tea. It seemed her doubt a moment before was no more. I had never seen her in a mood of protest. Her idiocy was getting absorbed in sympathy and passion. Perhaps for that she has been able to forgive all. She knew the home was not hers nor were its inhabitants . I didn't reveal this before. Had I done you would not have felt sympathetic with mother. Sister Nilu is my aunt's daughter. As my parents remained barren for years, someone suggested to my father to adopt her so that good luck will follow. Uncle didn't object. Sister

Nilu entered our house as a goddess of good luck` The happiness of our family that had halted at our threshold entered our home with her.

Mother was filled with rainbow's colour. The feet of the goddess of wealth and lotus flower were visible dinstinctly.

Mother's feet appeared to be the feet of goddess Laxmi. Father was surprised. A dawn of prosperity had waited to spread the news of delight, as it were. Sister Nilu's indentity got shadowy as much as that news of a possibility started gathering visibility. Nobody could decipher what happened. The wood pecker at the other side of the window sounded more strongly.

Things ran smoothly. A scene indicated an untoward event. Uncle dragged sister Nilu away. Grandmother had said to me time and again that all relationship got snapped.

Niluapa(sister) returned after so many days. Not being accompanied by her mother. Grandmother was no more. Father caressed her face affectionately. Everyone remained speechless. That silence indicated how much father loved her.

- Let me serve you rice. It's already late. Please take it`

Niluapa's face appeared bright and content as she heard this. She did not feel a sense of destitution any more.

- I have returned from college after classes. I shall take food when I come again. Daughter would be waiting for me. She spoke gently.

Unusual silence prevailed. Perhaps she forgot what to speak after this. She handed over a bag to sister in law and said, 'Please give it to Dipa.'

She touched mother's feet; descended the stairs like a stranger.

She ramined untouched till brother's arrival. He got some hints about sister Nilu's presence there and irritatingly said, 'What did she want to take?'

Sister in law silently handed over him the bag. A sense of surprise prevailed on the floor, on walls and in our minds too. A book emerged from the bag. It had father's photo on its cover. We were startled. What did the book contain? Some unpublished stories of father, his reminiscences, or his letter! What did this voluminous book contain? Who shall I ask?

Elder brother became almost a statue. Sister in law sat in a chair. Mother's indistinct voice pierced silence. May be she desired to know what the book contained. She desired to talk to the man of her heart. But could she? Light spread everywhere. Darkness disappeared. Characters in the book came out of it and started strolling in the room. Someone had put on a cap, while another held a prop. Someone was painting the sky, rainbow and the woodpecker.

The house exclusively belonged to them, as it were.

It was not possible on my part to decipher why such things happened. But I marked from the next day the golden fountain pen adorning my brother's pocket had disappeared.

And he had also forgotten to walk as father used to walk.

The Darkness Personified

I won't say now anything about the first two letters . But now I hold the third one in my hand . Incomparable time of wonder and incrediblity.

Mother's eyes have turned into an ocean of tears, as it were! Her cheeks have flooded in tears. The hem of her saree is getting soaked. She is speechless though she wants to express something. Almost stunned is she. There is none to console her. She heaves a deep breath expressing her griefs accumulated.

One feels surprised when one looks at mother's tearful face. What stuff she is made of, one can't but wonder. She shed tears so much when sister Nilu got married and left for her grooms house. She did n't stop though father consoled her a lot. Her tears expressed visibly her grief and disappointment. Her sobbing continued till midnight for many days like the tone of an unknown bird.

She was hesitant that one shouldn't give one's daughter in marriage at such a distant place. It would take seven hours to reach there. Even no relatives' houses were near there. How could one gather information about daughter's good and bad so easily? So her objection to father's decision was not at all irrelevant.

It will take only an hour from Phulanakhra to reach there. A car ride along the Niali road will reduce it to two hours. The family was aristocratic. Our son in law's father retired recently. He ownd landed property. His only son, our son in law, even serves at Bhubaneswar. Moreover, our daughter will not remain at the village.

Just eight days after the nuptial ceremony she will stay at Bhubaneswar. At a house rented by son in law. I have also seen the house. Father expressed.

Though sensitive, father failed to perceive mother's mind. Perhaps sister Nilu's ever smiling face, always brightening was indistinct to him. Not to change his decision, he said again gravely, ' The boy is not that bad in appearance.'

Sister was ten years older than I. My class five examination was over. So nobody prohibited me. Either I played or drew pictures in my drawing note. Sister had given me some colour pencils. She asked me when I was drawing pictures, 'Had you accompanied   father ... ?' May be she wanted to ask something more. But she withdrew her attention on me and remained looking at the branches of the mango tree overlooking the window. A cuckoo sat in its foliage.Branches of small mangoes had hung, manifesting all prospects. She didn't know whether such a charming scene awaited her there. After a little while she asked, 'Is there any mango tree?'

I could not remember if I had seen any such . How can I recollect because I sat beside father and gazed at the sparkling watch in his hand without any fun. Even then a flower vase made of Kaolin broke into pieces. Of course, I had no fault. The flower vase fell on the floor when someone pulled plates of sweets. Someone chuckled and cleaned the floor noiselessly. As if nothing had occurred! At that time I had gone outside.

Somebody, very tall and thin, had stood at the other side of the door. He had put on spectacles of thick lens.

- What's your name? - pressing his lips he asked.

- 'Shasanka'. I replied and didn't like to utter my full name.

Such unwillingness was quite natural as I didn't like his face. His eyes behind thick lens didn't betray signs of affection and intimacy.

- What do you think? Don't you remember? Sister Nilu asked.

Indeed, she was quite foolish. She could have asked me straightway about her future husband. Instead she asked me if the place had any mango tree! And if I said 'no', then she would ask again if butterflies flew there.

I turned inattentive and thought what I should do. Sister Nilu's dishevelled hair flew in the wind. Her eyes were filled with wonder. I could n't decipher why father was going to give her in marriage. I was not at all convinced that mother would get rid of worries and anxieties. But who would take me to school? She used to leave me on the school campus. Moreover, she was prosecuting her college education. What harm was there if she married after her education?

Sister's visage expressed distressful signs. Her looks exuded a caressing gesture. She would never get angry with me. Very indistinctly she asked, 'Did you not see a flower plant in their courtyard?'

I failed to make out what she said. So I cried and said, 'Nothing there other than a bespetacled pair of eyes.'

She drew me to herself. Her body was full of fragrance. Some drops of tear fell on her saree. I could't know why she trembled inside herself.

It was quite natural for me to be taken aback.

I didn't know she was so weak. She used to stand first in running competitions of her college.

May be she needed a little bit consolation.

Absent-minded and woe be gone, mother entered the room just at that moment. No language or sobbing could express that state. She wiped her face with her palm and asked, 'Why are you here? Would you eat or else I shall throw all away?'

Something in the room appeared colourless and grey. Perhaps sister, at that moment, accepted father's decision as inevitable.

Her eyes got wet.

Freeze, television set, bedstead made of teak wood, sofa set, almirah, dining table, dressing mirror - all kept on the verndah. A wrist watch of Shiko company and gold ornament were kept secretly in an almirah. The watch radiating blue light appeared rarest.

Father felt much worried as the day of marriage drew nigh. He would pull out the list of articles written on a piece of paper and see it time and again. At last a Bajaj scooter was added to the list.

Mother turned reconciled. Auntie reached five days before the marriage. She arraanged things necessary at the marriage ceremony - an earthen pot, a winnowing fan, unparboiled rice, round betel nut, coconut, earthen lamp, a small jug made of bell-metal, a low stool, cloth, etc.

In the crowd, sister Nilu got pulverized. She was searching in the room, as it were. She looked inattentively at the picture drawn by me. But she was totally speechless. So was mother. While she arranged books and notes on the table, her eyes glistened. She cast her glance here and there and drew out a blank sheet of paper.

I didn"t know what she wrote on that sheet - a song or poem. She couldn't draw the pictures of hills, the sky and rainbow as she didn't know how to hold a pencil.

An early winter morning. Trumpets blared. Concert by five musical instruments assured sunshine in the midst of indistinct fog. That would brighten path. Sister Nilu will leave for her in law's house by that way nurturing all love and faith. Perhaps mother was shattered inside; she was vanquished. In an unusual voice she said to father, 'It would have been better if I had seen the groom.' A very funny objection.

Time to begin the usual way of life. No more did mother say anything but father could hear her sobbing. It was so suppressed that only father could hear.

The groom's party arrived at midnight. Fireworks and crackers were burst. A conch was blown; women ululated; priests chanted mantras.

A canopy had been drawn under the mango tree. Below that was the altar round which plantain trees had been arranged. A holy pitcher had been placed there. A small pit to burn sacrificial fire was also dug. Fire was lit . When the bride and the bridegroom circumambulated such holy fire it was visible sister Nilu had not a wink of sleep. Her eyes were swollen. She appeared like a statue made of stone.

Mother appeared sulky. She didn't look at father at all. Nobody knew what thought rankled her mind.

She was no more able to bear with that crowded atmosphere. Father deposited another basket beside the basket of sweets.

- What do you put there? She asked lowering her face. Father appeared confounded. Falteringly he said, 'Nilu's books, her manuscripts of poetry - she will continue her studies there, write poetry too. I have kept in the basket all her poetry books .'

Mother felt comfortable with these words. However

at first she was taken aback, but then she got delighted and looked at father.

- She will raise a family. Continue her studie, write poetry too. Pray to God to bless her with happiness. Nothing else do I want. She said.

Father became stupefied.

A happy life - is it so significant? What does happpiness connote? What is its matrix? Perhaps sister Nilu was in quest of mango trees, flower garden, butterflies just to enjoy a little happiness. Various kinds of sweetmeat were packed in polythene packs. Articles such as bedsheet, almirah, packet of books were kept on the truck. All constituted sister's dream and future.

Niluapa caressed me while leaving.

Her loving touch possessed me for somedays. Her face soaked in tears had possessed me too. She could sob like a mother. Her cries could make time promiseless.

It was already my part to envision all such.

It had created before twenty years an invisible scene of wonder.

That scene danced in my mind now. Because I found sister's letter in the trunk as I was in search of our documents of lease and receipts. Sister Nilu's letter bore her calligraphy and the stamp of some lines of feeling of pains as well.

It created curiosity; quite natural. But what had she written? Though the inland letter had turned pale, it had not lost its content of sorrow altogether. Did sister Nilu swallow so much sorrow in her life? Though the matter seemed unusual, it was true.

- None understands me. I have been suffocated inside these four walls. They oppose my further study. I have lost all possibility of writing poetry. If I write poetry, they think I love someone. How is one imprecated with such a heartless fellow unless one is luckless! Suspicion and hatred only. In absence of love and affection, wealth is meaningless. Always shouting, and quarrelling. Threatening, and assaulting every now and then. Pray to God to stop his shouting. In fact, unbearable. I shall die. How long can I hide the bruises on my back? In spite of my previous two letters, you didn't take me from this place. This is my last letter.

Father was no more. He had left many days before. Things had turned reminiscences. No more was there time of hope and faith. Many a time mother had heard of sister Nilu's weal and woe. So tears welled up in her eyes. Slowly she said, 'I haven't read this letter. I don't know why your father had hidden it in the midst of land records and books. As far as I remember, he was ill at that time. He felt nonplussed during those days.'

At that time I couldn't say to mother I would travel to Keonjhar by bus that night.

Sister was putting up at Keonjhar. In a trembling voice she asked me over telephone two days back to go there. Had she met with any mishap? She didn't speak that. How could a woman afflicted with pain for long express it? After so many days she learnt how to embrace reality. That's why I couldn't know her mental agony and remorse.

Her residence was not far off the bus stand. So I walked to that place. It was mild cold. The moon was in the sky. A stray dog appeared feeling sleepy in the midst of slight darkness.

The door opened as I pressed the calling bell. Niluapa stood on the other side - her eyes glittering like stars. She looked at me with a daze, then she dragged me inside.

- Sleeping tablet has been administered. He slept just an hour before. He was ok. But suddenly he said he felt headache, strolled inside the room and struck hand on the table. Some mental disorder, I thought. Admitted to a nursing home. The CT scan confirmed my conjecture. Cells in head were defunct.

I felt sad and leaned against a chair. She gave me a glass of water and said, 'I am confounded. Know not what to do. He will come round if a reputed doctor at Cuttack treated him.'

Untoward incidents happen in life and perplexe it. In fact, all hope for a healthy world - fulfilled. They await a bright sunrise.

I had never thought of witnessing such a scene. Why were sister's eyes tearful if the world had meant to make a life happy and charming.

- Not possible to understand what he says now. He appeared to be groaning. Quite unacceptable. Previously he would be angry and shout but in course of time I became impervious to it. Passed post graduation, got a job. Wrote poetry. Even a poetry book of mine was published. I don't know if life can offer any other happines than this! After a pause, she continued, ' I acted against his dictates to build up myself. But complete silence prevailed in the last two days. Won't his words be understandable? Not for me but for him I solicit. How long can a person shouting always live speechless?'

Sanghagara falls was at a little distance. The sound of its crystal water was heard. Soft wind blew.

The stream of life flows like this, otherwise how could I overhear the fountain stream? Indeed a strange matter.

I looked around. Niluapa's poetry book and flower vase were on the table. A moment to get startled. Like the vase broken many years back. Its colour was bewitching. It looked bright in the mysterious room.

Indeed incredible - a girl ignorant of holding a pencil could draw the picture of life so beautifully! I couldn't believe how she was able to make her life filled with grief so picturesque.

Niluapa looked beautiful. Like a goddess. I felt things would be all right. Days of adversity would be no more. The voice of an intimate person would be heard. Her disjointed world be quite contrary. Her mind's full moon beams would be resplendent.

- 'Your last letter I got from father's trunk while rummaging documents relating to our landed property. Father had hidden it in a poetry book.' I said in a low tone.

Her face shone like a clear moonlit night.

But I could't ask her about her first two letters.

What had she written therein? As she had learnt the art of living, was she interested to know the mysteries of those lost letters?

Habitation at the Frontier

The snowfall has continued unabated for the last three days. Snow gathered on the road porfusely. Life-usual - has been arduous. The sky, green pine groves and patrolling military vans, appear faded. Intense cold has compelled shutting of doors and windows. All moribund, dejected. The city of Jammu appears to be a white canvas. May be Suchitra did not wait for such a scene. She thought snowfall will start. So sorrowfully she said, 'Mother, snowfall continues.'

Mother, in the other room, was busy arranging bed. Finishing it she came to Suchitra and said, 'None keeps bed disarranged as you have done. Arrange when you wake up. See, you will be married after fifteen days. What impression will they carry on you if you do like this?'

Suchitra looked at her. She presumed, mother didn't arrange bed, rather she tried to set right her incongruous habits. For the last few days, she has pestered her with instructions to learn the etiquettes of a bride. But she has failed. So she is getting confused more and more. She won't enjoy much freedom after marriage - she knows. She looked at the TV screen and asked, 'What's the colour of the sky?'

The answer to the question was neither emotional nor encouraging. Mother was surprised. 'Blue' - she answered.

Suchitra laughed loudly. Mother's face looked red. Her answer was not at all wrong. Yet she hummed the word again properly like a school kid.

- No, mother, not the colour of the village sky but of Jammu and Kashmir where snowfall has been continuing for the last three days.

Mother's face looked insensitive; she felt suppressed within herself. Because her world was different and contracted. Not at all colourful as that of Bhubaneswar. Her village, scattered and hesitant, was eighty kilometres away from Bhubaneswar. Her home was there where she had an assuring indentity. As it had green corn fields, mango groves - they have still preserved her unwavering stance. Even though the road had become a concrete one, whenever she visited the village, she would draw her veil. Her father and mothers in law were no more. Still the presiding deity, a stone image of Lord Radhakrishna at home was being duly worshipped there.

But for father these were insignificant. Many times he had reasonably stated to sell the village landed property. But mother would object. She never accepted the reason of selling that it was distant to look after. However, she was clueless about who would take care of it. May be she had no solution to it. Therefore, she would stare at father speechless. And that convinced father it was not so easy to be alienated from the soil. Hence habitually he would visit the village four to five times. There he would put articles in order, clear soots and dirts. Photos in glass frame and walls after being cleaned would look fresh. Mother used to draw pictures on the floor with *jhoti* and read Laxmipuran drawing veil on her face.

It was not possible for her to go to the village after father's demise. But whenever she introduced herself, she would never forgo to describe her village. And regretted she was unable to go there.

But Suchitra had no similar background. So her love

for village was impossible. How could green paddy fields, mango groves attract her being! But if asked about the colour of Bhubaneswar sky, she would look at it to answer correctly. Here the sky changes its colour in the midst of the untrammelled assembly of banners and hoardings. Mother grasped the connotation of Suchitra's expression. So it was meaningless on her part to reply. Hence she could repeat emphatically that the colour of the sky is blue.

She heaved a deep breath only.

The picture of Jammu was withdrawn on the TV screen. A debate on the Rafeal fighter jet had started . It continued in angry language and quarrels. So Suchitra was disinterested to see all this attentively any more.

Mother interrupted , 'See, invitation cards ramain undistributed as you say nothing. Let us go to Puri and offer a card to Lord Jagannath,. then invite your uncle. But I am immobile as you keep mum. Do you know how many days remain for the ceremony?

She was grateful to all, as it were - earth, the sky and God.

Suchitra was studying in 1st MBBS class when father's accident happened. He fell off the scooter. However, not a drop of blood oozed. But he fell unconscious. Breathed his last in hospital after he was kept in ICU for five days. Everywhere Suchitra felt the darkness of grief. Was it so easy to find a path in such deep darkness? But mother didn't lose heart. She stood strong for the family. When relatives, kith and kin maintained distance, she turned stronger and bolder. Not at all an easy matter. But such adverse ciucumstances embolden man. Perhaps he gets power to challenge. Had it not been so,she would't have agreed to the marriage porposal. Perhaps she felt obliged to herself also. Her secret sobbing indicated father's absence. Were he alive, preparations for the marriage would have been better, more dynamic. After distributing invitaiton cards she waited for the happy moment. May be she had learnt a little from him. She was teaching that very normally after Suchitra's return from Hyderabad. Time is not devoid of prospects though it seems all is lost. The reason is the soul and relationship. Affinity is a picture to be drawn on earth very gently, beautifully and fearlessly.

The next scene was usual. Suchitra didn't react and turned over an invitation card. It contained the marriage programme. Inscribed in golden colour. She got thrilled. A strange thrill had accompanied her from Hyderabad. It admitted with thrills the moment in her life should never be thrown into oblivion.

Suchitra was on duty that day. May be she was a bit agitaged due to some responsibility. A youngman introducing himself as Sanjay, stood in her front. Of course, two days back she saw his photos in the matrimonial profile. And talked with him too. But she was taken aback for his dramatic appearance. She felt the earth trembled beneath her feet and in her heart of hearts.

After twenty-five minutes they visited the cafetaria. Suchitra sat in his front. Sipped coffee a little. Held conversation punctuated by unusual silence. She couldn't remember what paintings had been hung on the walls there. May be of the sea or of a temple! But she remembered it was just twelve past fifteen. A moment- happy and fulfilling. How could she forget it!

Sanjay laughed gently and said, 'I was at home, so I could meet you easily. Shall return to Delhi and then to Jammu. We are not entitled to many leaves. Yet I could spend time with family. I am stationed at the frontier. So I have realised life more.'

His utterance, strong and convincing, overwhelmed Suchitra. Men   living at the frontier might be different. They were fearless. Sanjay appeared before her like a portrait. She could accompany him in the world. Could walk the rest of the path. Sanjnay could offer her promise to walk miles and miles.

A sudden shower fell on earth and vanished in the air. Suchitra got wet. She could see no more the unknown sky over her village and the everchanging sky over Bhubaneswar. After Sanjay departed, Suchitra was sure she would enjoy the sky at the frontier where the snow bathed earth would look bright in stars' company.

As Suchitra remained unresponsive, mother left the room.Not monologue but fill the growing trees in earthen vase with some courage and sympathy. She felt, as if they could be stronger because of the touch of her hand. As if their green foliage would appear energetic and glossy and start blossoming for a world of posibilities. But she was failing for the last fortnight. Who knows why Suchitra didn't understand her and why she could not also draw pictures of worldly affairs on her mind's courtyard!

Could she learn now how to wear sarees properly as she used to put on dresses of light blue colour? One would laugh the way she had put on saree and sat infront of her father and mothers in law. However they were happy. None could listen to what her mother in law spoke to her indistinctly and caressed her cheeks. But her gesture confirmed she had appreciated her son's choice.

Mother became happy too. She strolled inside the house treasuring her happiness. She went on arranging Suchitra's attachee everyday putting silk sarees, glass bangles vermilion and a copy of *Luxmi Puran* inside it with copious delight. For Suchitra's good luck, she also put the stone of a ripe mango. Suchitra would plant it in her in law's garden.

Mother had brought the stone of a ripe mango. Father had planted it. It has grown so big that its top is not visible through thick foliage. Now deep red mango buds hung emitting sweet scent. Honey drips in drops. It has birds' nests. The playful fights of squirrels are seen there. Defying all this, green mangoes hung from its stalks. Nobody knows when they turn red like vermilion brushing themselves against fog. Residents know when they are ripe. Their taste is sweet. This year the boughs here drooped more being burdened with a type of ripe mango called *Latsunderi*.

Mother decided to send a basketful of such mangoes to Suchitra's house. It is believed a woman eating that sort of mango does not lose her husband before her death.

It was natural on Suchitra's part to be startled.Because Sanjay was at the otherside. His face looked clear on the mobile screen. He was in military dress, a cap on head.

What do you think? he asked without any anxiety.

Suchitra was at her wit's end - found no answer. She was in a state of bewilderment. In fact she thought of him in the last three days; visualised the topography of the frontier. Also she was drawing pictures of terrorism in her mind. That's why she was in a state of unconsciousness.

- I am heading for Rajori. Shall talk to you when reach there. If not, be not worried. Be not sad. Well, have you distributed invitation cards? He asked eargerly.

- I shall do it after I show you. Just look here, how do you feel? Is it good?

Suchitra held an invitation card before the mobile screen. But Sanjay's face disappeared all on a sudden. So Suchitra couldn't know if he had seen it. But that silence indicated he had seen it and was glad too. Sanjay had just waited for this. Not that the card looked good but it had become an unforgettable emblem of faith and love. Suchitra felt that no moment was filled with helplessness. She chuckled.

- Mother, get ready. Let's go to Puri and invite the Lord. Then some other proaccupation will follow. Don't delay. I have no time - She said while entering the bath room.

Overwhelmed, mother glanced at her. She didn't know Sanjay's had possessed Suchitra in her absence.

The car took almost two hours to reach Puri. Mother touched her head reverentially at the Lion's Gate and entered the temple. Crossed the twenty two steps. Behind the Garuda pillar, Suchitra's face looked contented and fulfilled. The Lord too looked serene and assuring. Mother anxiously handed over an unvitation card to a priest . She said, 'Please touch it to the Lord's feet. It will bring my daughter all luck. She willl enjou a happy life.'

In a solemn atmosphere, the Lord's *aarati* was being performed. Indeed, a surreal moment. The priest returned with that invitation card on which was a garland of leaves of the holy Basil plant. Loudly he said, 'All your misfourtune will be averted. You will be blessed with goodness. I have prayerd to the Lord for this.'

Mother folded her hands humbly to pay homage to the gracious Lord. Suchitra forgot what for she should pray to the Lord. She came out to the Grand Road through the Northern gate and looked at the *Nila Chakra*. Found no sky. There had spread lighted darkness. She felt utterly suffocated to spend more time there in the midst of crowd, loud shouts, rows of shops and *nirmalya*.

May be a lump of darkness had waited behind the mango tree. She opened the room. Her mother's mobile rang when they were entering the room. Sanjay's father's tremulous and halting voice at the other side was heard.

- What happened? What? It was mother's voice unusual, inaudible and almost sobbing.

Suchitra took the mobile from her mother. Heard some inaudible words. It was a terrible moment. She fell on the sofa. The entire room was filled with so much impenetrable darkness. Felt some bombardment inside her. Everything crumbled. Branches of the pine tree, grass and a cap appeared flying. The snow appeared red.

Darkness prevailed in presence of electric light. Darkness behind the mango tree trespassed on the room fearlessly, as it were. Nobody's face was visible. Mother switched on the TV, came to know there had happened blasting at the frontier. No, it had occurred in the room, as it were. In such a moment one could not console the other. Mother kept on looking at Suchitra, just to avoid that terrible sight on the TV screen.

Suchitra sat motionless, eyes closed. She had no courage to witness. The entire atmosphere could be so terribly disfigured and ugly - she couldn't think. Everything appeared disintegrated and sorrow-stricken.

The news read - Major got martyred while making IED explosion ineffective. O, may such news be fake!

He looked at the setting sun at the frontier. His uniform was not blood-soaked, rather he was liberated because of the colour of the graceful dusk. He was absorbed in meditation. Wild flowers around him scattered fragrance. No, not a trace of burnt earth was there. All - false.

Should someone meet with such death!

Suchitra had seen death on hospitalbeds many a time. But she had never felt broken, she had felt no sorrow. She had taken it all as normal. But now she got splintered inside her and got soaked in tears. There must have occurred an earthquake. Her dream world got ravaged. There was no sky for her nor earth under her feet.

How would the silk saree, glass bangles, vermilion, the book *Luxmi Puran* and, invitation cards be useful? She had learnt the etiquettes of a daughter in law. How would it avail her? It is believed a marriage depends upon perfect match of two horoscopes. So is also an auspicious moment. Was it that auspicious moment in her life? Had the marriage been performed fifteen days before, she would n't have been confined to the ravaged house hopelessly, awaiting a morning sans light.

O, how lucky it is to live at a frontier! It is a charming and overwhelming moment too. May be she was not destined to experience that moment.

She hid her face with her palms and asked mother, 'How far is Rajori?'

Mother had no answer. The night appeared prolonging in the thick foliage of the mango tree; in Suchitra's trickling of tears, no question of living at the frontier.

The Fixed Star

Perhaps this much was enough - a bundle of sticks of hibiscus cannabinus, wicks soaked in ghee, drawing of a house with powered rice, some funeral cake made from powdered rice to be offered to ancestors, offering of food to deity placed in a plate of bell-metal. Grandmother used to lean against our mudwall on which were drawn pictures with the liquid of powdered rice. She would sit slightly bent. Yet she was vigilant about everything necessary for offering our oblation to ancestors.

Mother was busy arranging flowers in the picture of housedrawn with powdered rice. She would keep ripe plantains on leaves of jackfruit tree, burn incense sticks, place cynodorn dactylon, unparboiled rice, a small jug filled with water, an earthen lamp, and a bell.

Father would chant mantras that penetrated darkness, as it were.

Ancestors in another world - famished and thirsty - must have waited for this throughout a year. Once they were in this world, moving here and there and were devising plans to keep body and soul together. They remained as actors to usher in future and possibilities.

Since long grandmother had left us. Father followed her. He was quite well. He had gone somewhere, came back, sat on a cot, complained of headache and breathed last. Nobody could know how the last breath departed. This has remained a mystery with me. Otherwise how could I see that oily scar on the mudwall that still shines in spite of smears and smudges.

You can't comprehend this easily. How many would admit they have comprehended the connotation of relationship? One finds rude soil everywhere having no possibilities. Although a seed of expectations is planted, two green leaves can't penetrate the soil and come out to sing the Bhagbat of relationship. Because of dearth of water, air. Things appear queer and incredible.

Two days back.

Mother rang me up. She stayed in our village. Like grandmother she looked like bent after father's departure. In weak voice she said, 'How could the death anniversary of ancestors be celebrated this year? You didn't listen to me but proceeded to your daughter's house. Things would not have been like this, if your father were alive.'

May be she was getting shattered inside. The earth that emboldened her to stand firm was no more below her feet. It had got shrunk. Undone, she would want a refuge to sustain herself. She would lean against it. I heard her crying. She wiped tears from her eyes.

- Listen, this is an annual ritual. Our ancestors would be waiting for this. But you...!

She could't complete. Did she want to speak something more? Or did she not deliberately reveal more?

What can unravel one's sorrow hidden in one's mind? She was helpless; may be she could n't bank upon the home she lived in. She remained as such always suffering from the fear of helplessness. Such fear frightened her more after father's death. She became absentminded. She would shed tears that incarnated her grief. Apparently it was a moment of being shattered. Alone, she thought darkness was her constant companion. None except herself was there in such a large house. Quite impossible to live alone. However, she continued living, watering plants, raising pumpkin creepers to the roof with a support, sprinkling ashes on brinjal leaves, intending that the possibilities embodied in greenery be not infested with worms.

Indeed it was strange.

In spite of my repeated requests she did not leave home to accompany me to my residence. What did that home contain? Except solitariness-quite rankling. But I would feel it quite uncomfortable to stop even for one or two days whenever I went to the village. I would feel suffocated. Feel the presence of so many shadows on walls, corners of doors, courtyards playing hide and seek with themselves, as it were.

Mother was fond of sarees. At times she would show me her sarees preserved in the wooden almirah. In fact the green saree having pitcher embroidery was her most favourite. She would touch it emotionally time and again. At the time I would get enthralled to see as if a shadow entered the almirah. But could she see that scene? No, not at all. Had she seen, she wouldn't have chosen a path to lead her life apathetically.

I got lost in myself and said, 'Be not worried. I shall perform that ritual here.' She became happy and said enthusiastically, 'You don't know the mantra. So invite a priest. Hope, Odia priests are available there. You will see how your ancestors would be satisfied when you perform this. You will be blessed along with your children.'

The last part of her utterance convinced me she had no sense of dejection and indifference any more in her mind. She was sure her ancestors would be offered annual oblation and their souls would not remain thirsty anymore.

Also her words indicated though we lived at a distant place, we were not alienated from each other.

I became conscious that there was little time to arrange all this. I was at my daughter's house at Hyderabad. I was not much acquainted with it. Here the language was different and customs as well. Moreover, daughter in law might take it otherwise. I felt disappointed . Things appeared painful to me, Sunanda got irritated and said, 'I had cautioned you much before. We should have come here after performing that ritual, But you never heeded me.' Sunanda's words made me more helpless. Realised I had committed a mistake. The fine, attractive Hyderbad appeared pale and colourless. Its well-adorned malls, magnetising lights, sky-kissing towers of different companies appeared insignificant. I felt this city also suffered from disappointment and pain like any other small town. It also contained grief and remorse. Here also lived in despair thousands of youth who had come here with a hope of getting employment but in vain. Not that they were unemployed but they would feel helpless, insulted and confounded because none understood their language.

I felt restless and found no way out of it. My face bore marks of anxiety. Could I not perform that ritual? Saw mother's pale face at a distance. She was crying. As if she tried to find the hem of her saree to wipe her tears.

Sunanda could mark my helplessness and said suddenly, 'Like the characters in your stories you are bewildered but emotional. I have not asked our daughter. She will take us to a man when she returns from her office. The man, an Odia, is the owner of a hotel. Very near. He can give us the whrereabouts of a priest.' Her words surprised me, I didn't know how suddenly my sense of despondence would disappear. Mother didn't wipe tears from her eyes with the hem of her saree. Rather she touched my face and wiped the sense of my despair. I felt relieved, as if a waft of air blew.

Daughter returned at nine pm. Before Sunanda said anything she said, 'Let's go outside for dinner.'

I didn't take it to be so important but Sunanda was waiting for this. She changed her saree in no time and looked at me smilingly.

After a few minutes we drove our car. It appeared rows of shops, lights, traffic police, coneshaped cases ran backwards. Time too. We felt asif the night was not late and the sun set just now. But time eternal couldn't contain so much shout. I felt as if I had entered a strange, helpless world without my knowledge. I did not know where it ended.

In spite of being busy throughout the day, our daughter looked lively. She got down the car and said, 'Let's purchase lamps first. These are sold here.' We entered a shop and found all our required articles there. I had never thought these would be available so easily. The lamps were very beautiful. Many hands touched their lips and bodies. Indeed they looked like human beings. Strange in shape though, they were attractive. But those were of no avail. They were not earthen lamps. I was in quest of a lamp like which mother used to light at doorstep. I touched it with my finger. Experienced a strange experience beyond the real world.

All noise became silent by degrees. As if the earthen lamp touched me passionately! Indeed a hand! An experience many years ago. Pages of the past got unrolled before me. I was surprised. I felt I was getting drowned in a fathomless sea, as it were. Like a branch of a tree about to bear fruits. I felt unsteady in wet sand, as it were. I had forgotten mother had sent me to purchase an earthen lamp. I was unable to see anything. Someone's muddied hand lifted me and made me stand on the verandah. Not that it lifted me but actually moulded me again by her healthy hands. I felt ashamed in my heart of hearts as my face, hands and legs were smeared with mud.

A voice filled with wonder shouted at me, 'How are you here? What for? Your entire body has become muddy. This is a muddy place.'

Frightened, I said, 'Mother has sent me to purchase an earthen lamp.'

She rinsed my wet cloth, washed my hands; mud turned watery and got washed by her fingers. She stared at me, wiped my face and hand with a dry towel.

The soles of my feet shook.

- Had I got news I could have taken all these. O, did my pal send you here? How stupid! What do you want to take?

Lo, I have nothing to feed you. Well, do you like eating ripe guavas or ripe papayas? I shall pluck these with a long stick.

Whatever she spoke, that flowed from her ambrosial consciousness. My aunt Magi was getting metamarphosed to Jasoda, as it were. While caressing me again and again she was getting absorbed in a unique experience. Gradually her voice turned soft, filled with affection.

She was very often the butt of quarrels between father and mother. Consequently mother would not be talking with father. Father would prefer to remain silent. However, after a few days aunt Magi would visit our house. She would get lost while assisting mother in her domestic chores. Our home was always encircled by wonder and pain. Mother would say, 'None was present at home at the time of your birth. Only for your aunt Magi I survived. When I opened my eyes after delivery, I saw her holding you in her hands. She was barren. Yet she had profound attachment for all. She would never be angry even if reprimanded profusely. She would visit you smilingly even after two or three days.'

What for was she greedy? She has already placed before us creamy milk, ripe papaya and a sweet cake - all constituting a basket of love and affection.

She belonged to a potter family. Whenever she shaped an earthen pot, she would shape a man, it rumoured. So people crowded in front of her house. But why should she care this? She thrust into my mouth some creamy milk with a spontaneous emotion. She was beside herself with joy. After feeding me, she wiped my face well. She said, 'Let's go. I shall take you to your home and ask my friend why she sent her son to purchase an earthen lamp in such a scorching afternoon. That too on such a day! A witch hovers around this village.'

She picked up my hand and paced onward as if she swam in space. I ran with her, breathless till we covered the distance.

- Hello! Haven't you chosen a lamp yet? Useless. I have bought all. Hold this bag.

I got freed from aunt Magi's clutch, as it were.

Sunanda could mark my state of self-absorption.

Something continued flying in the gentle wind.

I asked, 'What about the priest?'

- That has been done. Daughter has contacted him over phone. Don't worry. Very good. May be our daughter was worried about my anxiety. So she devised ways how to perform the oblation ceremony well. So I had no complaint against time and the town.

The priest arrived on time. He had a red towel on his shoulder, marked his forehead with sandal paste. Sunanda was waiting for him. It was a small room. A square was drawn on the floor with powdered rice. Leaves of the jackfruit tree and flowers were kept in order. Incense sticks were burnt. A carpet was spread.

My face eastward, I sat.

Sunanda lighted the lamp.

The priest started chanting mantras to invoke and concecrate deities.

I had to utter the names of my ancestors. But I did not remember their names. Had mother with me, she could have remembered those names. Like grandma.

- Offer the oblation of rice balls inside the square, put betel near it and let drops of water flow against your elbow and fall on the rice balls.

Water, dripping from a sacred blade of grass, was offered for the thirty deceased souls. They were corporeal having no organs. But they had deep desire to be content. I am alive and devising ways to remain alive. But they don't get ways to be born again.

Shapeless shadows appeared in the midst of the smoke of resin. A piece of cloth was placed on balls of rice. He invoked those ancestors - May you arrive in darkness and depart in light. May you roll on the twenty-two steps at Lord Jagannath Temple.

Since we believe in such inalienable relation we are obsessed. The priest explained it; departed he contented.

I am unable to speak anything about such relationship. But my daughter asked straightway, 'You told us in our childhood that man becomes star and twinkles in th sky after death. Grandfather must have been a star. Could he have come to such a distant place?'

Silence all around. Loneliness too. In a strange resplendence, the star remained fixed like an incredible joy.

Good-for-Nothing

This story contains another story. I feel uneasy whenever I tell it. Silence encircles me. The environment turns solitary. As though none existed there. Sunanda's presence becomes superfluous. All this, notwithstanding, I hear a cry in distress waiting for me at the otherside of the door. Like an assassin. Though I know him not, he tries to break into my house.

- Where are you from? What's your name? What do you want? Sunanda asks.

No possibility of getting a reply from the assassin unknown. I admit, it is not a matter trifling. I should obstruct. But I fight shy in the teeth of any adversity. So naturally I become repelled. The assassin's face appears as ferocious as that of a tiger - his physique black and yellow with terror; his sharp nails emerging from his claws. I hear him growling.

Sunanda' eyes are welled up in tears. So is his uncertain future.

You may think, I shall relate to you my first story. No, that won't be. Because that may make you dejected. It does not contain any extraordinary incident which would thrill you. Undone, once I tried to relate it. But words couldn't keep pace with me and characters appeared phantasmal, strangers.

Ten year back.

I remained unemployed at home after post-graduation. Preparing for interviews. Stacks of book, relating to competitive examination were on my table.

I kept some paper cutting and certificates in files. Not that I had not faced interviews three to four times but in vain. A shadow of disappointment engulfed me and my family too. My failure made my father pessimistic. His look would indicate I should have shouldered the responsibilities of my two younger sisters. But could I do? I was performing well in written exams. But would fail in vivavoce. Someone cautioned me I won't get a job. Without recommendations, one shouldn't nurture any hope for it. This may not be rational for you. But I got shattered as I failed to get a job. Also I had no courage to meet friends. I was failing in competitions. So I used to while away time in a park. In the midst of crowd. Shadows of trees would create a weird atmosphere. I felt I did not belong to that world.

May be I was getting shaken, obsessed with a thought that all roads were closed for me. I was surrounded by dense forests and mountain-passes and felt darkness at the blaze of noon. Shrank inside in a state of helplessness.

In such a critical time appeared a scene unusual. In the darkness of night father was standing near the gate. Was waiting for me for a long time. I didn't know what was time then. Because my batteryless watch was defunct before some days.

A moment of utter helplessness. Father spoke in a low voice, 'It's of no avail if one gets disappointed. Diligence and perseverance bring good luck. You have prepared the door. Oneday you would hear knocking at it.' His words got lost in darkness. Some last words of his were almost inaudible. What did it connote?

There was a verndah; two rooms were adjacent to it.

Then there was a door. At the end there was a water pipe. Drops of water dripped. Not easy to know if the soil or the house was thirsty but I knew the house had no promise. Its cracked wall made visible-wants, grief and hunger.

I had no time to think who would build what. But I perceived someone's hand shaped the soft lump of soil of my mind with conviction. The round lump of soil was becoming thin by the tip of his finger. Its upper part was setting down by the hands wet. A faith, getting shattered, was assuming a fine form. Was it an effort of one to build oneself?

Stump of hair was visible on father's face. He bore a weak physique and unkempt hair. While entering through the gate, I could know he was quite strong in spite of this. The earth under his feet was powerless to shake him. May be, he was shaken inside for sometime. Hence he forgot what to tell me. He was unmoved.

A chair on the verndah had a towel on it. Father closed the gate after he heard the chirping of a bird feeling sleepy. Very gently he said, 'A marriage proposal for you. I have tried many times to speak to you about this. But have failed. They know that you are unemployed. Yet they agree. My friend staying at Raygada is known to them. He says the family is quite good and the girl...'

I did not know the matter would start and end this way and bring me an unimaginable moment. Father stayed put. Should he ask as he used to ask 'Where were you loitering for a long time? Have you taken meal?'

However, such questions were irrelevant now. Father appeared quite different after mother's death. It was that evening. Mother was quite well. She was humming the Bhagbat in our prayer room. Father could not know when she halted. Why her voice was heard no more? How long would she be in the prayer room? He was worried to start for bazar. To consult her about the articles to be purchased, he entered that room. Silence prevailed there. Mother had fallen on the grond, the Bhagabat had also fallen from her hand. Father failed to decipher what had happened. This much he knew mother had departed silently.

Every morning father used to sit in chair and read newspapers while mother plucked flowers. Chanting mantras she would roam about the flower plants till her basket was filled. Father would sit in the chair till she finished plucking flowers. Now the chair with a towel on it remained unoccupied . None sat in it.

Everything appeared an uncertain possibility in shadowy darkness. I said in a controlled tone, 'May be the family is good. But I won't agree so hastily...'

Father's face got intensely darkened. For a moment he looked surprised - a helpless person. Had my mother been alive, he could have cousulted her to know any other means to convince me. But the way of his life was quite still. None was there to talk to. Because of his teachership he had suppressed a lot of anger, grief and anxiety. Hence he used to say to be good man or *sthitaprangy*.

In darkness of the night that very pitibale and perplexing moment passed.

But the next morning was not at all happy for me. It dawned with a world of remorse and worries and strarted rivalry against me. Undone, I was compelled to take a paintful decision at last.

A winter morning at the Rayagada railway station. Darkness unknown hid in foliage. Very cordial hills spread like palms of hands. Greenery all around. I was alone, an air bag on my shoulder. I had never begged for anyone's compassion. I banked upon my ability to compete in examinations and get a job. Similarly I was not willing to get married on someone's recommendations. However, if I did not obey, father will feel sad. That's way, I was there on a winter morning. And I decided to decline after I met the girl.

The train halted. Someone dressed neatly, approached me. Smilinglyhe started conversing with me. Then we got into a vehicle. He was living in quarters at Therubali, his place of service. He asked if I faced any inconvenience during my journey. I replied in the negative.

- There is a hotel nearby. Let's refresh ourselves there first. Then we would start for their home. They must have waited for us - he said.

I felt sleepy and needed some rest. But couldn't. As the scheduled time drew nearer, I was haunted by a strange fear. As if I was going to sit for an interview! After getting refreshed, I felt it quite uneasy to turn the pages of a newspaper.

Their home was situated near the college in front of Collector's residence. We entered the house. I saw some paintings on the walls. Some books were visible in an almirah. Who was reading these? I thought. Straightened my shirt and sat on the sofa. At this moment, the girl appeared removing the curtain. The room became absolutely silent. Beads of sweat spurt on my brow. I got confounded. How could I begin? What shall I ask? Moreover, how could I decline the proposal by saying the girl was not beautiful and that's why her parents agreed to marry her with a youth unemployed.

But I never expected a dramatic scene was awaiting me. The scene presented full lips, glistening eyes, a fair physique, quite shapely and attractive. I had not seen a more beautiful girl anywhere.

- How much sugar should I add to tea? - she whispered.

I smiled and thought tea would be sweet without sugar .

Her face turned bashful and lips more passionate. A whiff of air entered through the window, a sort of tremulation spread throughout my being.

- Have you read Pablo Neurda's poetry? I asked. The question was absurd altogether. Why should one read Neruda's poetry? That too love poetry? Would she love and marry by reading much poetry? What thought absorbed her? The tea cup in her hand got shaken. Some drops fell on her saree. Whether or not she knew the scar was indelible so easily. So she left the place to wash it? He did not want to lose the mement.

Through a brief conversation, I could know she was not after plenty. She just needed a few things to keep body and soul together.

She just wanted that much. Not Naruda's poetry, rather my stories.

Her father said, 'We all have read your book.' I didn't know till now I was one of the characters of my stories. The being vanished behind the curtain; she had known me since long. That accounted for my presence here.

I was startled.

I could n't go to Therubali. Spent the next hours in a hotel as I was suffering from an ache in my waist. While returning, I assured my father's friend I must visit him when I come again. I shall enjoy the woodland there. In fact, I was convinced there was nothing for me, everything was at Raygada - happiness and life.

I realised where happiness existed after Sunanda wedded in our house. That life could be so brimful was beyond any imagination before. Got my appointment letter after fifteen days. Lecturership in a college. Leaving father in the village I came to Bhubaneswar with Sunanda. We lived in a rented house - very spacious; a flower garden in its front, a papaya tree beside the boundary wall. The garden was gorgeous with green plantation leaves. Life's possibilities got expanded; at midnight stars looked bright through the window.

But God knows why Sunanda's visage turned pale, though the stars were amazingly lustrous. It appeared she was in search of some thing lost. She would turn absent-minded whenever she plucked flowers. She was quite disinteresed to read my unfinished stories kept on the table. At times she also didn't look at me well. Not to speak of talking to me. No dearth of anything in our house. A very shocking state which no language could explain. Her gestures indicated she did not want to be hugged or kissed. So what actually she desired? Not she, rather I myself was getting buried under a sort of pathos.

Returning from college oneday, I found the house dark. It presented a house of phantoms. Sunanda, sittng in a sofa, didn't look at me at all. She objected to my presence, as it were.

- 'Switch off the light' - she shouted as I was switching it on.

I turned impatient with her expression. Annoyed, I said, ' Why do you shout? What has happened to you? Life would be defunct if you behave this way.'

- What else have you presented me to make my life functional? Don't you know the messages on the mobile?

- Messages? - gently asked I.

She sobbed and said, 'You have copied a story.

Its characters and words tally with your story. This news has been out in newspapers.'

I stood still and sat down being imprisoned by a moment of grief and calumny. I thought I would say to her that after reading that story I was engrossed in the fragrance of a *mahul* flower . Its character resembled you. She had herself built up a writer's house. I was confounded how could another writer transcribe my experience?

I was already afflicted with endless regrets. Now it got aggravated with dejection and pain. I couldn't give vent to it, was caught in the harsh clutch of insult I said, 'I was unable to write stories for so many days. You cannot feel the grief due to the inability of writing. Had read that story in same magazine and enjoyed it. Thought I shall get rid of a suffocating state if I could write the story. Know this. It is said a literary creation is the result of 'sadhana'. I pooh-pooh such an idea. It's a blatant lie. You can't visualise that in an intuitive eye. Though it appears as bright as a distant star, it's completely obscure.

Sunanda failed to read my mind. Simply looked at me blankly. I thought - was the world filled with hatred, malice, and jealousy? Was there no mean to get rid of it? Was it not possible to journey easily to an environment, free from shouts?

Time passed. Yet the darkness inside our house persisted.

In an assuring gesture, Sunanda told, 'Why do you worry about it? You confess to your guilt, you would see things will be set right.'

I looked at her intently - did she advise me or sharpen a weapon against me? I was in a fix. But this much I realised I should shut the door. Had father been there I would have asked - Father, which one knocks at the door - good luck or bad luck?

I had not visited home for many days. How could I know, whether he still sat on a vacant chair.

The sky was star-studded, everything bright and detached. Could I visualise that sky if the door was shut? There would be darkness enerywhere.

Slowly I said to Sunanda, 'Don't open the door if there is knocking. The assassin is at the otherside. I know him. Only a persen-good-for - nothing - like me, can occasion such an unpleasant occurrence.'

Sunanda said nothing. She arranged carefully the sheets of paper containing my incomplete stories and caressed the characters therein. 'Be not nervous. Stories will not remain incomplete. Again either you will laught or cry. We are starting for Therubali tomorrow. Therubali - full of *mahul* trees. You are in charge of this house. Be cautious not to love each other. Nor would you read Pablo Neruda's love poetry.'

Dramatic

Improbable it was. So soon Bimala would be blessed with a contented world so easily and she would be overwhelmed! Breathless, she came out of her house; looked, with surprise and dependable sight. Then she caressed herself with a soiled piece of cloth. She was overwhelmed with emotion and affection. Indeed, it presented a wonderful scene.

What did the scene contain so that Sukanta shouted? May be he didn't want a moment like this for him.

He asked, 'What are you doing?'

Was Bimala really at fault? Tears welled up in her eyes spontaneously. The world around appeared lachrymal. Sukanta's face appeared hazy in the midst of *sal* trees that had shed leaves and a bicycle - grey with dust.

Even after seeing the bicycle, Bimala remained unconvinced. The bicycle leaned against the trunk of the *sal* tree like a dry branch. In fact, Sukanta had purchased it from the market. What was its cost? In wee hours he had left home in a huff. Not paying any heed to her importunities. Dorps of dew dripped from *sal* leaves on wet grass. Bimala too has felt wet with sadness and sulk since then.

Their quarrels continued for the last seven or eight years. Consequently she would live frightened in their home. Most importantly, whenever she protested, Sukanta paid a deaf ear. That would surprise her as to how she tied the nuptial knot with such a person! And lo, she would live with him throughout life! A person sans love, sans wealth.

Admitting his helplessness and inability Sukanta said a while later, 'This is an old model. Its brake does not function, its chains rattle while paddling; its seat torn. Since it sold at a cheap price, I bought it. Have to spend some money on its repair.'

Halting for a while he said, 'It's a ladies' bicycle. Just mark, how its rod is bent. Knowingly I purchased it so that you would ride to the bazar.'

Bimala wore a sense of surprise on her face. Sukanta wiped her face with his towel and said, 'Hey, why do you look at me this way? I shall train you within two days. You will accompany me to your workplace. You will paddle while we return. I shall be on its carrier, rear seat.'

Bimala's face got flushed. Air inside the house swayed fully. The chirping of an unknown bird was heard at a distance.

Sukanta emphasised a lot on the bicycle. But where would it be kept? They had a two room house. - one their sleeping room and the other for their kids. The verndah was used as kitchen.

- Where would I keep it? - asked Bimala.

A relevant question, indeed. While turning side at night, many times she had placed her leg on Kalia's body. Hence he had cried. That had indicated those two rooms were inadequate for the three. Moreover, Kalia was already seven years old. She has never complained about the necessity of another room: Rather, while she leaned against Sukanta's bosom carefully, she felt the room was not safe for love.

It was not a matter to be spoken so easily. She wiped

her sweats and said casually, 'Instead of purchasing a bicycle if you had built a room, I would have reared a herd of goats.'

Her words were not accepted. Sukanta turned absent-minded. The painting of red flower on the wall, pumpkin tendrils creeping on the roof and the growing maize plant competing with each other beside the fence were not visible. These were insignificant for him. Did he desire to earn more and live happily?

Satirically he said, 'You are unable to bring a bicycle from your father's house but you dream of a house of three rooms! How silly! I won't complain from today. God is the only saviour. I shall ride to the bazar and earn wages by virtue of my labour there. Do you know, the wage - three hundred rupees for a day's labour.'

- What! three hundred! - These words were pregnant with immeasurable wonder. Yet it filled Bimala's mind with illimitable confidence and strength that she was not distressed. The stream of her life would flow free. At any moment she could go to bazar with Sukanta sitting on the carrier of the bicycle. She will labour there with Sukanta and return to her thatched cottage at dusk. There would be awaiting them a world - intimate and delighted with brimful passion.

The moment of utter helplessness and hopelessness disappeared.

Bimala lifted the cycle by her hands and leaned it against the wall of their cubicle. As the cycle handle brushed against the wall some portion of it fell on the floor.

Sukanta followed her and stared at her too. Sunanda said, 'It would be here. Don't distrub it. The cycle is mine. Do not feel sad that my father was unable to give one. Is not your thing mine?'

Sukanta moved about the room and was surprised.

Bimala demanded nothing more than that. She was happy with what she had got.

Indeed it was an overwhelming moment when rice was cooked in a silver pot; potato was burnt in fire, *kankan*(a vegetable) plucked from the orchard was fried. Sukant's face got brightened with a smile while he chewed the fry of *kankan* with chilly served in a silver plate. Perhaps that indicated there was neither grief nor remorse anywhere in those two rooms. Only gratitude reigned there. The story of such happiness could be read from the arts drawn on the walls of mud.

Indeed the contented world is not colourless.

It was early in the morning when they woke up. A blackbird twittered. Pattering of the *mahul* flower was heard. The herd of goats bleated in hunger. Kalia cried. No more would any dramatic event happen so easily.

A cloth bag was hung carefully around the cycle handle. The cycle chain was greased with *pongamia glabra* oil. The seat was covered with a colourful piece of cloth. The carrier was made spick and span. Sukanta couldn't know when Bimala woke up and did all this. But this much he knew - gruel rice, the fry of *kankan* vegetable or green chillies and a pinch of salt were in the bag.

When the cycle ran, it produced no rattling as before.

Softly said Bimala, 'Buy some sugar. Tea dust is no more , no articles at home. Buy all these with your wages. Yes, sister Sula comes today. Do whatever you like.'

It was very difficult for them to make both ends meet. Sometimes they ran short of sugar, at other they had no milk. But their wants were invisible because the could cook rice. However, wants persisted. Because of want of money he was compellled to purchase an old bicycle. But its paddle didn't move well.

And lo, sister Sula would visit at such a critical moment! What would she demand - a red piece of saree embroidered with flowers or a goat?

Sister Sula's village was located after three villages. Hers was a stooping thatched house of mud walls. Yet she did suffer from wants as he suffered. She possessed cultivable land ; her children were able to work; one of them was employed at Bhubaneswar. Kalia would be glad if she visited them. She must have brought with her either carambola or ripe banana. At times apples and papayas.

Sukanta forgot he was riding an old bicycle. Its break was not working properly. Cars, jeeps and trucks were moving past him along the pitch road. As if they competed with one another!

A terrible sound. Instantly one of the cycles had slipped to the paddy field and the bell had slipped off the handle. Breathing was slow. Blood oozed from wounds. The shirt was torn, legs lost chappal. Rice, the fry and green chilly had got scattered. Not a trace of salt. Sukanta's stout but useless body lay beside that. He was unconscious. Frightened, the bird had hidden itself among the thick foliage of mango trees. It produced no chirping.

May be all was over. Who can survive such an accident?

Bimala was stunned when she saw Sukanta on the hospital bed. Should a man leave this way! How can he depart before discharging his duty of building another room? Who should she bank upon henceforth?

After a struggle for twenty days, Sukanta could sit on the bed. He stared all around. Bimala failed to comprehend what he babbled. Sister Sula was beside the bed.

The doctor explained slowly, 'I have prescribed medicines. Take it at the counter. Regular medication will cure him fully. Nothing to apprehend. Meet me after fifteen days.'

Neither distress nor illimitable perplexity persisted any more. Prospects of his recovery drove away all illness. When Sukanta boarded the ambulance his weak legs appeared immobile. After he reached home, his utterance turned more incomprehensible.

What did he say? What did he demand before Bimala like an obdurate child?

Bimala was terribley worried - what to do?

She fould it very difficult to tide over such a situation. Just after seven days, sister Sula desired to leave for her home. In tearful eyes she said, 'I am detained here so long. Things there might have been destroyed. You know everything - he suffers from night blindness. At dusk he gropes only.'

The world suffers from so many problems. Now upon whom would Bimala depend? Nobody was for her - neither God nor relatives. She burst into sobbing. Said, 'He would quarrel everytime. Never did he purchase a piece of saree at any festival time. On the other hand, he would taunt - go to your father and get a piece from there. Now he is unable to speak properly. Damn, I want to take revenge.'

Bimala couldn't believe her ears - what Bimala said. Sister Sula left for her house silently. Bimala had no vegetable or maize at her home to fill sister's bag.

A dramatic scene after a week.

The bicycle ran on road - Sukanta was sitting on its carrier. His weak hand had clasped Bimala's waist of course. Bimala was losing concentration at times. Then she was getting down the cycle and arranging her saree. She was not impervious to any grief. So she prayed inwardly - Let not the running of the cycle be stopped. Yet her cycle carried the load of grief of the entire world.

The Shadow

Ten o'clock already. No time left to wait for the lift. She took steps and it took only eight minutes to reach the ground floor. She felt breathless. Her plapitation was uncontrollable. Sanjay may be waiting somewhere here. He would be annoyed to see her and ask, 'Was it so urgent that you descended by stairs?'

She would laugh; her lips would look red. She would act like an actress as if she got fatigued. Forget, at that moment, her laptop, e-mail, conference, manager's order and her illness.

She looked around asif she was in quest of a star in dark night! It was not easy to know which was her dearest star. Because all would look like a lover's face - intimate to the core. Hey, what did she think! Even a year after marriage she was in quest of stars, love and a handful of dream. She felt asif her head reeled. She was weak. Though she drank some glasses of fruit juice, she felt terribly thirsty` She recovered from dengu ten days back. She was ok. While busy in the office, she felt unbearable heat. Her face appeared swollen. Frightened, she rushed to a nursing home. From blood test it was diagnosed not a common fever but dengue that had caused heat. She felt nonplussed. She was powerless, as it were. Speechless, she simply stared. But Sanjay put his hand on her shoulder asif he assured her. Before hand, she had felt desolate, she was left to herself and solitude encircled all around the world.

She fell off the chair, though bright light was burning. She was overpowered by indifference, a moment of dejecton. Her eye lids closed welcoming a barren future. Though she emboldened herself that nothing bad would happen she was getting liquefied on the floor.

She had never imagined to meet with such a moment. Sanjay's face looked indistinct. Almost crying. None was there with her who could caress her face looked indistinct.

Mother lived far away. Father was afflicted with anxiety and apprehension always. He had no courage after his retirement. That's why she had disagreed. May be that was an unusual decision for him.

But she had surprised all when she firmly said, 'None but Sanjay I shall marry.'

It created a moment of snapping all relationship. Father would protest, she thought. And that would result in an explosion at home. The four walls won't be able to uphold the strong roof of relationship. The abode built of brick, chips and cement of love would crumble into pieces.

However, no such scene was seen.

Father had left the room gently. Sunanda had failed to read the language on his face. But the way he paced, made it clear that he was helpless and aimless as well. He found no words to counter her unforgivable crime. Mother had heaved a deep breath due to overwhelming grief. She cajoled her and said, 'Look, nobody should say what you said. My darling. Please study your father's mind. He stayed at so distant a place...' Her sentence remained incomplete. It was a scene as good as dying from apprehension.

No doubt, mother would rush as soon as she heard

of my illness. But what of father? How could he manage there? He had been dependent on her throughout life.

He was unable to keep the disarranged clothes in order, rows of book would gather dust; his unfinished stories would remain as such and their characters would be forgotten.

Sunanda's illness aggravated even at the clean nursing home. Her blood pressure dropped day by day. She felt sleepy always. The saline dripping from the plastic pipe indicated she was breathing. She was alive and saw an inconceivable dream. - A little girl with a satchel hanging on her shoulder was running after a dappled butterfly in a garden of different types of flowers. The butterfly was getting distracted. It flew from flower to flower. The entire garden was the entire world, as it were.

Somebody's voice at a distance cautioned her not to stumble.

A dream like this had Sumitra dreamt at the nursing home during the last four to five days. Sanjay was beside her always. As she opened her eyes, she saw a contented, happy family had awaited her at Miratmet. A place not very far off Hyderabad -About a distance of fifty kilometres. Its shopping centre is seen sparkling during night. Its buildings are sky-kissing. The sky appears entangled along the metro way. This road running a long way is connected with the future hope of a large number of persons. Though it is assuring the star is not visible in bright light.

While returning from her office Sunanda would be in quest of the star. Miratmet was surrounded by green forests of tall trees. Yet the star was visible through the foliage of those trees. Not an insignificant matter. Perhaps that was the reason why an invaluable portrait of relationship was painted along the pitch road, encompassing tall trees, the hill and the star.

Who was the artist? Whose voice was heard that aimed at overwhelming the girl running after the butterfly?

To be helpless and assailed by accelerating anxiety are quite usual in life. But who would show her way? May be Sanjay stood somewhere. She cast her glance around again to find him out.

Sombody stood beside the pillar in semi-darkness. He/she had been looking at her sharply for a longtime like a ghost. May be it was a mental construct. However, she was frightened and proceeded to the gate hastily. She was fully unable to get rid of the indescribable fear. She stood silently near the security guard. At the moment she heard clearly Sanjay's voice. While she was sitting in the vehicle, Sanjay asked, 'You are too late!' While driving he looked at her face. But his look had almost no modesty.

He asked, 'Don't you feel ok? Would you drink fruit juice?'

- No, she replied. Though the reply was brief it flung endless grief and dejection. Like a winter night getting shrunk more in cold wind.

What more could Sanjay ask? She felt parched in her mouth` She was weak. She experienced burning pain in her heart. She had no strength to uncork a bottle to take a drought of water. She stared outside because of the crowd and loud shout she heard there. Their vehicle screeched to a halt. She failed to understand what had happened. She got off the vehicle and witnessed an incredible scene.

An adult gentleman was shouting queerly, pointing at the rear part of his vehicle, indicating the amount of damage it had sustained. And the damage must be compensated for in form of cash. A frightened youngwoman stood near the vehicle. She was clad in a punjabi of blue colour. Her eyes had already bedimmed with fear. It was obvious while driving she was not attentive. As a result the accident occurred. Speechless, she cast a hesitating glance all around.

Sunanda didn't know her name and her whereabouts. Yet she felt she had seen her face. Like the star. Gently she moved to her. Uncontrollable were the young woman's tears.

May be she had never imagined she would meet with such a moment of accident in the city of Hyderabad.

Sunanda cast a careful glace all around and asked, 'What's the matter?'

Slowly the young woman replied - 'While I was moving my vehicle backward, the accident occurred due to inattentiveness. However, his vehicle has not sustained much damage. But he claims twenty thousand rupees. I have no money with me now.' The aged gentleman was becoming uncontrollable. His words and gestures didn't appear normal at all. He was determined to display his anger and protest, as it were. Dramatically he said, "Proceed to the police station. The matter will be settled there. You will tell your name and mobile number too.'

There were scratches at several places on the body of the vehicle. Politely Sunanda said to the gentleman, 'If you claim, you will get compensation from the insurance company. Why do you compel the young girl to go to the police station? It's very late night!' Even a relative would not have extended such deep sympathy. Sunanda was very conscious of what she said. So she said again, 'Hope you understand what I said. The young girl won't go to the police station. Rather you would go. Because you have put a girl into trouble in the middle of the road at night.'

The environment fell absolutely silent.

The gentleman stood dumbfounded. As people became aware of their own concerns, the crowd dispersed. Some vehicles left the place. So the place looked vacant.

A worried lady approached them. She was quite clean and could decide how to face such a situation. She said, 'See, he is mentally upset. Since our daughter eloped with somebody somedays back, he has been haunted by an unknown ghost. So whenever he meets a girl on road he wants to know her name and her mobile number.'

Sunanda was startled. She never imagined such a strange pathetic moment would be created. Like a destitute, the gentleman moved towards his vehicle silently. The lady had clasped his trembling palm.   As if she was cautious that any unthinkable incident won't happen again and none should feel glad to see her mental agony.'

While returning to the vehicle, she saw the young girl following her like a bewildered insect. Nothing to fear now. Nor was there a moment of repentance. Her eyes sparkled like stars.

She said almost indistinctly, 'Sorry, you are late only for me. But were you not here...'

She was still haunted by a sense of helplessness. Her tears and grief were quite visible. She was very emotional and clean inside. Sunanda clasped her hand, and said freely, 'Please keep my mobile number. Talk to me when you reach home.'

Certainly it was an optimistic moment. It was foolish to worry about some trifling fear that existed in a lonely town as inevitable as a darknight.

The young girl collected Sunanda's mobile number. But she appeared she was in search of something she had lost.

What was she searching - moment, words? She said in

a voice suppressed a little , 'I drove here to meet my boy friend. He has come from Mumbai. It's late night. My parents would be irritated. I shall talk to you after I reached home. Please say at that time that I was attending a birthday party with you.'

With her eyes absorbed, Sunanda looked at her for some time. She thought she was reading a story for a long time, as it were. She didn't react. Silence prevailed in the car. No fear of losing anything in the lonely night.

The young girl's face was quite clear. It was radiant and it expressed an overwhelming emotion inside her. Apparently the moment was content because it achieved something.

Sunanda had awaited such a moment, as it were. She sat beside Sanjay. Life is love, nothing else, she thought.

Slowly the moon rose in the sky.

The evening looked beautiful and mysterious.

Her mobile rang, just at the moment. Mother's call. She was suffering from insomnia. She would remain awake till midnight. Would go on looking at old photographs in album. Or else she would write songs secretly. And hum those alone. In father's absence she had kept hidden the manuscript of her old songs in an almirah. Like a priceless possession. That too wrapped in a silk saree.

Have you reached home? She asked.

Sunanda remained silent. She was confounded. What should she say? What a misfortune she had to encounter today!

She would relate a story starting from the phantom to the young woman. Is it so easy to pitch yarn?

Father appears like a shadow when she writes a story. It is very easy to compose on the unsafe existence of daughters. That's why she has done it throughout her life and has hidden the manuscript of her songs.

Sunanda was unable to tell the story. May be she was sick - inwardly and outwardly. It seemed her breathing increased unimaginably. She looked at the star-studded sky and said, 'I am with Sanjay. Shall reach after fifteen minutes.'

The Incompetent

It was unpromising rain. The earth looked stunning by its drizzle. There rose a slight storm of dust. Clouds vanished in the pageantry of torn sheets of paper, dry leaves and colourless flowers. I opened an umbrella to get absorbed in the betwitching turning of the love song of the rain drops. But where was rain? Perhaps rain loses its capacity to create a sense of intimacy where life is lonely. I was ill in mind and body. For some days past, I was experiencing a burning pain. I felt it painful to set my foot on ground. May be it indicated paralysis. I had no desire to come. But I came as I knew my future would be insecure if I didn't. So I came. The path bore a lot of footprints.

I got a letter three days back. The letter related an event. When I was serving another branch I had committed some irregularities, so why I should not be duly punished - the letter asked me with an order that I reply to it within fifteen days. It was a matter before five years. I was clueless about it. Moreover, I couldn't remember every bit of the matter.

From Cuttack to Kamakhyanagar - the distance was covered within one and half an hours. At two sides of the road were green paddy fields. Immense wealth swayed; still water moved, as the shadows of cranes got reflected in its mirror. It looked like a sheet of drawing paper. Mango trees also stood beside the road-energetic and amazing. However, my fear had grown much worse than my pain. In fact, I can't express it. I felt the touch of someone's hand on my shoulder. The environment got charged. The pictures of solitariness disappeared. I remembered the thatched houses of mud walls, where raindrops used to drip from the roof.

I was bathing in it without ever apprehending I would get cold. A moment of affection and emotion. Afterwards my eyes turned red and -fever attacked. No remission as if it had started mighty enmity with me. Father took me to a doctor. The doctor prescribed some medicines and advised blood test. I felt afraid. What was I suffering from? A sort of fright spread throughout my body when blood was drawn from my body with a syringe. Darkness and soots of discomfort encircled me. I felt suffocated. A whiff of air got stuck in my heart. I shall die. Surely, like grandmother had died.

The report brought father joy. He said, 'It's only viral fever.'

I looked at his face and suspected perhaps he told a lie in order to inculcate courage in me. If he was right, why was not there remission? Moreover cough also persisted. My entire body was weak. Footprints of insects and worms were visible around my study table. Indeed, they had arranged a picture of denying my existence.

But my fear was finally unfounded. So father said, 'What can you do if you fear so much? You have many miles to go in life.' Even his words could not free me from my unfounded fear. But I tried to lead my daily life without any worries and anxieties. For that the boundary of my life extended a little.

I looked around and turned absent-minded. The bazar had changed. No temporary cabin was there. Buildings had sprung up. The shops were lighted and well decorated. Rush in photo studios. Adivasi women had crowded there to have their group photographs necessary for applying for loan.

None could recognise me. Quite natural, as I was slightly bent onward due ot lumbago during the last few years. I have used more powerful lens. Hair on my head has thinned. Kept my umbrella in the car and shut the door. The sky was clear. My toe was trembling in the shoes I had put on. The toe in my left leg was trembling more. Heaved a deep breath. I was ill. Could feel the ghost of reversal accompanying me. Slightly bent onward, as it were.

The table, chair and the faithful almirah appeared familiar. So was the bunch of keys in the almirah. My stay there was for a year. Then I was transferred on promotion. The mementos awarded to the bank during my tenure and kept in the almirah looked more brilliant.

Pushed the glass door and entered inside very slowly. The manager stood and complimented me. He was my colleague in another branch. He smiled and said, 'The zonal office has sent letters to four persons including you. Mr. Mohanty visited our branch here and verified our documents, register and other papers yesterday. Things have become so complicated that one has to be careful while working, Otherwise one would invite trouble.'

A whiff of breath spread in the room; it appeared, he was a complete stranger who did not know me and was never my colleague also. He rang the calling bell. Very cautiuosly entered Pramod. Though his face apeared bloodless, his dress was neat. He smiled as he saw me. That indicated he was still loyal to me even after so long.

He was about to say something when the manager said, 'Please serve coffee to Sir; O, yes, inform the canteen, sir will take lunch there.' Pramod left even before the manager completed his say. He left as a bird flies.

- Sir, the branch is not good. Very difficult to manage. Brokers are loitering on its campus. In the pretext of granting loan they are exploiting adivasis. You were here only for a year and left without facing any trouble.'

His words were intended to praise my work - efficiency. Rather, I understood, he desired to be delighted by listening to some experience still unrevealed.

Eventhough it's not easy to study everyone's mind totally, I am able to study it to some extent. I may or may not believe it. That's different. But I realised it was very urgent to contain myself. If I turned naive he would be able to read my love, loneliness and agony.

I said nothing, though I handed over the letter to him. Perhaps he could know it was his minimum duty to show me all the documents relating to the loan.

But his face turned pale and he paused for a while. He drew my attention to another table in the room and said, 'Sir, all the documents are there in a file. I shall supply if you ask for more documents.'

His words were polished, professional, I felt . I smiled. But I didn't know how it affected so that his face seemed confused, as it were. His eyes behind spectacles got brightened. While rummaging through the file I happened to see the loan document. Startled I became. Didn't know what type of moon will rise today. But this much I could know the evening star would look beautiful at the village Gadapalasuni. More beautiful willl look the clear fullmoon night.

A scene before five years. Dense forest. Fragance of *sal*flowers floated from a distance. A fountain flowed nearby. Very adjacent to it spread a vast sugarcane field. Plantation of plantains was to its left. A canal flowed through it. Where it ended, there began a field where chilli was planted. The colour of ripe chillies made everywhere colourful. Leaves of maize plants were being shaken by the wind. Everything looked promising and full. I had never seen a scene of such overwhelming opulence of greenery. And that the earth could be so generous! But I was assailed by a sense of wonder. Then what was the crux of the problem? Why was the loan not repaid for so long ? The loan with its interest was getting multiplied. As a result, the bank marked it unrealised. Eventhough the earth was generous in offering vast wealth, loans were not being repaid. Was it deliberate? It was natural to expect a reply to this question.

But Sukanta Rout's face got creased due to confusion and helplessness. I couldn't understand what it meant - madness or a well-thoughtout strategy?

I visualised inwardly a scene of water motor, a tin filled with diesel, a wooden chair, four to five hens in search of their food in a vegetable plot, an asbestos-roofed house of two rooms, two to three plastic chairs inclined against the wall. It was meaningless for me to expect some more scares there.

The door ajar opened slowly by the touch of a young woman. It created a promising full moon night. I was surprised, excited with strange delight and unalloyed emotion. I was surprised that Sukant Rout's adversity and deparvity was no more his, that was mine. None here was unknown to me. They were known to me since long. Incredible was the moment.

The narrow house got expanded in the smell of a burnt maize as it were.

The wall was painted with portraits of many hopes and faith as it were. The feeling of depravity and disease, I felt before sometime, had disapeared. Suchitra, fair and buxom, stood in my front. She couldn't speak, her lips trembled.

She arranged her saree on her bosom and asked, 'Sanjay, since when have you been here?'

At first, I was amazed and then replied gleefully, 'I joined here before ten days. But I never expected to meet you here!'

I didn't think it proper to worry about what promises in life should one avoid. Rather I knew I could cross the bay of dream of reality. Suchitra, a peerless beauty, was reading with me. Candidly speaking, I fell in her love. She stayed at the women's hostel. We used to meet after classes without anybody's knowledge and presence. Because college campus was not that expansive, mango trees here were neither laden with boughs nor were they shady. Moreover the town was small. Though it was much inconvenient for rendezvous, it was very easy to be slandered here. To avert such disadvantage, Suchitra devised a plan. She would come to station by bicycle where we sat on a cement bench. There she would draw sketches with a pencil. The platform sheltered tired passengers; a frock-clad girl was seen there , a blind youngman sang. The sky and cloud above, I would sit silent as if I were alone, God knew why she said one day, 'Can love sprout this way?'

Probably I felt it difficult to fathom her expression. My gradually worsening efforts at strengthening our home and my future hindered to advance further on this matter. But she became a character in each story of mine. Her absence has been soaked in my anxiety and eagerness. I have wandered for her footprints when rains dropped.

What more than this can happen?

Indeed, I myself was surprised how Suchitra thought

love had no colour in spite of so intense love of mine, or else I was unable to drench myself in love.

One day, without my knowledge, Suchitra fled her hostel. She remained untraced in spite of a lot of endeavour. I thought if I got her whereabouts, I shall finalise the way. But that did not happen.

Now I happened to be in a similar moment. After so many days .

Suchitra sat in my front though not near.

She looked at the sky. What did she think to say? Would she beg forgiveness for her mistake? Even if she explained herself, none would take her explanation. I also sat at a safe distance.

- Would you please buy me a piece of saree?

Stunned, I looked at her face. It appeared as if drops of tears fell on her face.

- If not, then a gold ring. I passionately desire you would put it on around my finger.

There was much noise and hurry on the platform at that time. Damn, my thoughts!

Suchitra drew a beautiful picture sans canvas, colour, and brush. She was possessed by a strange thought.

She said, 'I didn't return to college to study anymore.'

We had lost everything as our house was burnt by fire. Our financial position was shattered and that weakened father mentally. He lost faith and strength. No way out. So we left Bhuban and are here. We are trying to raise cultivation again. The only way of earning. I admit, father has been defaulter. But we would repay the instalments as soon as we reap sugarcane . Hope you will help me.'

I remembered the disappointment in life. But Suchitra appeared otherwise altogether.

- What kind of help? I asked.

- Would you facilitate refinancing?

I only looked at her face steadily. The matter remained unfinished. As I was unable to assure.

Sukanta Rout had left the place at the beginning of our conversation. But I met him while coming.

He was busy irrigating his sugarcane field. The smell of burnt maize was still in my hand. He smiled, folded his hands and said, 'I shall give Suchitra in marriage after I sell sugarcane. I have arranged the groom. He is serving in a company in Pune. Please be not worried. I shall repay the loan.'

I felt lonely along the path running through Gadapalasuni and felt someone leaving me again. Got tortured. Since then I had never gone there. But Suchitra came to my bank and met me.

Did try as much as I could. But I failed to extricate myself from that memory. Went through the documents in the file and found out my irresponsibility - the mistake committed. I had not prepared the inspection report and mentioned it on the register. Negligence of duty indeed . Moreover, I had not issued a letter to Sukanta Rout to repay the loan within a year. So no follow-up action had been taken. So the letter to me for disciplinary action. The letter carried truth. But what could I do? I was terribly worried. I was awfully unable to forgive myself. I had already proved myself to be an inexperienced manager. Had I been careful about my duty, I would have been on safeside. I felt deeply agonised.

Pramod arranged the papers and kept the file.

The manager was absent. He was out to attend a meeting at the sub-collector's office before an hour. The room was absolutely silent.

In a tone almost inaudible, Pramod said, 'Sir, I shall tell you something.'

Perhaps I had no other way but to stare at him.

- Sir, Suchitra belongs to our village. She enquires me about you and is worried always as she couldn't repay the loan.

Annoyed, I said, ' If she was so worried, why didn't she repay the loan? You see, I have been served with a letter of explanation by the bank.'

Perhaps Pramod didn't take it well. He drooped his head and it appeared he thought to say something else . But could not.

I looked around and found none present in the room.

He said in a low tone, 'Sir, she is no more. Expired a month back. God knows what happened.'

I sat motionless in the chair. Thought how far was Suchitra's house from this place!

I had been there only once. You may say, I couldn't learn the art of loving and lost the possibility of proving myself as an efficient manager. For the first time tears tickled down my cheeks like drops of rain. Without my knowledge, I became a character of my story. As I sat in the car, love, loneliness and pain sat near me like my dear kith and kin. But I couldn't surmise who had placed his/her hand on my shoulder. It was not possible any more to penetrate the mystery in this frightened state of mind. Now you can ascribe one incompetent who waited for rain to initiate love.

The Corona Alarm

I never apprehended so calamitous a time in life like this. Twelve o'clock. My watch showed when I was already filled with various doubts and anxieties. On Tv screen pictures were changing exhibiting signs of uncertainty and helplessness on the faces of hapless persons.

Unprecedented journey of the people soiled with dust, bags hanging from their shoulders, cloth baggage in hands and all other stray articles in their dependable plastic bucket; Perhaps that's all their wealth that seemed strange.

They were not that anxious about their jobs; rather it was very important for them, how to reach their villages without protest and anger. They clamoured fruitlessly against injustice meted out to them. Also they were alienated from all due to impatience and fright. None extended them consolation. Nor had they any unreasoble passion to stay.

The distance from Hyderabad to Balasore; from Surat to Ganjam, from Lucknow to Haryana, from Maharastra to Patna, from Telengana to Kanpur. How far! For years together these luckless men had left their native places and stayed at far off places. Who should he put the question? In fact he was clueless. But this much he knew well his dilapidated village home contained so much beauty witnessing which his labour of travel would mitigate.

Indeed an incredible pageant. Capable of

transforming the contours of a face, if touched. As they covered distance banking upon such a peerless scene, they could get rid of fearful mental crisis. Instead optimism stretched from the earth to the sky. Like a full moonnight.

Their journey started since the lockdown was declared.

But my mother couldn't comprehend anything. Simply she looked at the Tv screen and appeared burdened and discouraged.

A spacious verndah; five rooms at its end - all neat and clean. A door near the last room. But mother was unable to cover this distance to reach the garden. Moonbeam trees, laden with flowers, had stooped and appeared to be a star-studded sky; the cape jasmine flowers scattered fragance; *champak* flowers smiled; chinese box flowers beside the boundary copiously bloomed. Father had planted all these while mother took care of them. She used to caress while watering them. And would initiate a dialogue with them so cordially,.That's why our garden was filled with so many flowers and so much fragrance.

The zephyr and the butterfly would lose path here. Did it afford happiness? I was unaware of its meaning. While alive, father would sit here till midnight; mother batherd in moonbeams. She looked like a little girl while she strolled along and across it.

Perhaps it is more delightful to show the moon to others than seeing it. That is the matrix of boundless peace. It would enable one to cross miles in the struggle for existence. All misfortune would be averted by this. Since the helpless man was aware of it he was eager to return home.

Was mother aware of this or not?

Some clatter was heard from our shrine. The door

shut, opened. A cat, hiding its face, disappeared at the corner of the almirah.

With a tinge of astonishment, she asked, 'What is Corona - a goblin or demon? Why should I confine myself to house to fear it? I can't go to the garden to pluck flowers due to its apprehension! Do you know, how my deity's visage looks pale without flowers?'

She was discontent with her expression. The lastpart of her expression sounded unusual. It appeared she was not afraid. Rather the faith in her would fade if she was unable to pluck flowers for years together. Consequently she would not be happy.

I explained to her, 'Corona is a virus that causes the spread of the disease. No medicine for its cure. It is best to be at home consciously.'

Stunned, mother looked at me. She asked, 'How strange! I shall ramain inside home, not talk to or mix with anyone! Even shall n't pluck flowers! what is this - disease or enemy?'

I didn't know how difficult it was to explain it to her . Said I, 'The matter is not that. You will be safe if you confined yourself to house. The disease will not spread. That's why I prevented you from going outside. And also ask you to wash your hands again and again. Do you follow me?"

Her voice of protest subsided and slowly she said, 'Yes,'

I could perceive her voice was choked in intense anxiety.

As she closed the door and went inside, I proceeded towards my newspaper office.

The road was awfully solitary - only two or three persons were seen. Their faces were hidden behind masks. Circles had been drawn in front of shops. The road was a geometry note, as it were. Everywhere social distancing was religiously maintained.

The police officer stopped my vehicle near the barricade. May be he couldn't mark the pass pasted on the glass of the vehicle. So he naturally urged me to show my indentity card. Of course, bearing my name and my office address, it hang from my neck in a green lace. He paid attention to my photo with slight hesitation and allowed my vehicle to run.

Neither the sky was cloudy nor was the entire world. But abruptly the wind blew violently from the Kathojodi side. And it started raining without thunder. Consequently the road was flooded. As my vehicle ran onward, the rainwater splashed up both sides of the road. Birds of different species started screaming on branches of *peepal* trees.

Through the gate my vehicle entered the newspaper's office. Raindrops fell off the leaves of *Kadamba* trees on the bonnet.

Time appeared shrunk. I was late fifteen minutes due to rain. No other way out except feeling annoyed with myself. Because any other thought than that was meaningless. In hot haste, I entered the room of the news editor - quite aged, hair on his head dishevelled, and his eyesight weak; So he used spectacles with thick lense. On the table in his front lay some files and paper cutting and his mobile of black colour.

He was not in a mood to demand me any explanation. So almost he ordered, 'The relief party has waited for you. Accompany them and prepare a feature on labourers. See that it bears a definite portrayal of their daily existence becoming unbearable due to lack of work. And the morning edition would carry it.'

I had no time to look at him helplessly. I collected myself adequetly and came outside. A vehicle of blue colour, surrounded by some press employees, had waited. Some packets of food and water bottle had been kept inside it. Some paper packets containing masks, and soaps were also there. A banner attached to its front side, was meant for advertising the noble deed of an organisation. Its letters were tolerably round and bright.

The sky was clearly azure Even it did not appear that a little it had rained cats and dogs just before sometime. The wind blew through *kadamba* foliage.

We got into the vehicle at 10 O'clock. But what was most important was that the sun shone brilliantly. Its shine fell on the earth straight way. Indeed, the earth is thirsty always.

- We have to reach there soon. The information says no relief party has gone there for the last two days. The situation is beyond control.' - said someone to the driver.

The vegetable vending zone had been shifted from Chhatra Bazar to Link Road. The shops in rows sold ridge gourd, parbal, some green, parbal like fruit and the bewitching greenery of the tender shoots of spinach. Someone had drawn a picture of greenery with his brush on the canvas of the pitch road, as it were . A jovial dog was loitering while the continuous voice of the police shouted. Our vehicle crossed all this and halted at the slum of roofs stooped, walls semi-dilapidated, and the soil under feet shinking.

Oh, the environment looked so ugly!

With the screeching of the vehicle mingled the plaintive cries.

It was not necessary to call any one. One by one,

they came out of their shanties almost damaged, nursing a hope they would be fed that day. It was quite natural for us to be emotionally moved. A state of utter distress not possible to ask anyone in the uncontrollable situation at that moment.

A pregnant woman came from the crowd and requested, 'Please give me another packet. One more...'

Perhaps none paid attention to her sudden request. Because all faces looked almost similar. Moreover, it was not easy to listen to a hungry person's voice. So the woman's voice appeared insignificant though she had collected much strength and courage to say so.

But I experienced a lightning in me. I handed over her a packet of food and a bottle of water as well. Stunned, she stared at me. She didn't know how long she stood stunned.

Gentle wind shook her state of dejection and restlessness. She looked at the root of the mimusops long tree hesitaingly and said, 'Sir, please come to my house very near this place.'

A dramatic request. Natural to be startled. The surroundings were not yet free from shouting. It was not possible on my part to know what another pathetic scene awaited me in that house.

A similar request again.

Her voice was very feeble and wavering - her face wrinkled with unmistakable disappointment and panic while her palms moved on her face and neck. Perhaps the hem of her unclean saree was ill afford to wipe her beads of sweat.

I could catch what she meant and said in a low voice, 'Let's go.'

I had never imagined such an insensible sight had

waited for me in the house - all filthy and flaccid. Inconeivable poverty spread every inch.

A silver pot pressed inside lay on the hearth. A plastic case lay open. Some remaining spices stuck to the end part of the case. A bicycle flap was also there. A world disbled was shackled lock, stock and barrel. There was none to take care of the house. Even if one existed, one was not present there. No certainty of his return.

A photograph fading gradually, hung against the wall - a youngman may be of thirty -three leaned against a sal tree, his eyes and face may have been totally burnt in the scorching sun. The room contained three to four tin boxes and a chair apparently not vulnerable.

She leaned and opened a tin box. May be there was some invaluable possession there. The clothes kept inside were disarranged. So were documents. From beind torn newspapers she brought out a book very carefully. She looked at me and chuckled. The chuckle was very familiar to me.

I was beside myself with such smile six years back. Almost bowled over.

A place full of *sal* woods, *kurei* flowers and sky-kissing hills. In a residential school at the foot of the hill, Charulata was a mathematics teacher. But I was almost bad at the subject. If one were disillusioned with addition and subtraction, one would be enxiety-ridden, I thought. As a result, one would stumble in advancing conveniences in one's life. That came to pass. Charulata fought shy of expressing her love towards me. She lived her life as per her whim. Remaining untouched by intense romantic passion, she was completely entangled in her livelihood.

I also thought it natural to touch Charulata's mind. I was employed in a newspaper organisation, spending time counting uncertainty now and then. Everything shaky, I thought. The entire world was sorrowful, things were getting alienated from one another - man from man, world from world, sky from sky, relationship from relationship.

Mother had not seen Charulata. May be you too have not seen her. Her bubbling eyes indicated they contained dreams and a soft corner.

What does a soft corner portray? A portrait of intimate love! I know not how to draw a picture. But I write stories. I have written many stories with Charulata as their character. Apparently this is a safe, happy action of mine.

I could know that when, as a guest, I entered that residential school. A romantic surrounding of *sal* tree, under their shade grew flowers of varied colours. Butterflies flew, the cuckoo cooed. Charulata had never seen me before, so intimately. Really an overwhelming moment. While speaking she was beside herself with joy, as it were. While introducing me to other guests, she did not forget at all to praise my creations sky high. The sense of delight and fulfilment writ large on her face transported me to a world beyond.

Indeed, it was a moment beyond moment. I thought, she had nothing more than this to convey me and assure that both of us would meet eventually, whatsoever. I can't say how much she had penetrated into my life then. But after two hours I realised the meeting was over. And I had to return alone along that impassable way in that dark night.

Charulata saw me off at the gate. A girl followed her. She was not so fair; had bound her braid with a white ribbon. The colour of her frock was almost like the colour of the balsam flower. She was singing song on the stage some minutes before. Her canorous voice enthralled the audience. I heard clapping in her praise. Charulata looked at the girl's face and said, 'Rebati sings and writes her mind. Her writing resembles your stories when read.'

I was in a state of wonder. I didn't know how old she was. But did she know hill, *sal* jungles at this age? Her knowledge of the cloud was quite improbable.

- 'Her daily life is miserable. She is motherless. Her grandmother at home is blind. Her father works in a kiln. A very miserable family. She depends on me.' Then she caressed Rebati's head. Rebati's eyes were brimful with tears.

I stood silently in that atmoshpere and said, 'I am leaving. I shall come again at my convenience.'

I had presented a book to Rebati while getting into our vehicle. She had felt surprised, grateful and chuckled.

I had never imagined after six years she would appear before me with the book sporting the same smile, and open the book and I shall read those three words to Rebati, affectionately.

You may not believe those three words turned to be a letter of her introduction. Her face was colourless, and she was alienated from the surroundings, in spite of having this book.

What stuff is life made of? Can she cry or can't? Perhaps she was blessed with that strength; Her life turned unfounded like a nightmare. She burst into tears uncontrollably. While wiping tears she said very painfully, 'I left studies halfway. Father didn't pay attention at all to what Charu didi said. Rather he quarrelled with her and struck off my name there and married me off within two days.

The marriage was pre-fixed. The illiterate Basu was one year older than I. He was also unemployed but had a hope of getting some employment. He brought me to Cuttack. One day he would get work and the other day he would remain workless. Somebody told him he could get work, if he went to Mumbai. So he did.'

Then she felt breathless, took a pause and said, 'I was on the family way. Hence I couldn't accompany him . Remained here. For the last three months he has not sent money. All factories have closed due to Corona. I am at my wit's end. So whenever a vehicle arrived here, I rushed to it to get a packet. And I aslo supplicated for another packet. I apprehend relief might be stopped tomorrow.'

Strange is the change of everything. The sky enveloped with cloud changes. The moon hides in the sky.

A life full of happiness and delight is soaked in darkness and tears. Myself was helpless. Yet said I, 'See, your difficulties will vanish. Government is making plans for you.'

With a little wonder Rebati cast a glance at me and expressed in an unsteady voice, 'These are not for us - the labourer class. Had our government been concerned about us Basu would not have walked miles beside the railway line to reach home. How foolish! To walk such a long distance!'

She said no more. Clutching at the fence, silently she stood. I was in search of some words with which a sympathetic sentence could be constructed. And if she heard it, she would be happy. In fact, she would get some means to keep her body and soul together. To be candid I was unable to utter such a word of assurance. My lips parched, as it were; my soul shattered, as it were!

I got into the vehicle. Admitted I was utterly helpless and weak in the teeth of the pandemic. I had no courage to extend her a helping hand, saying , 'Come with me!'

The road had no scene of wonder or thrill. Most of the shops were closed. In medicine shops were seen faces ridden with fear and perplexity. In those circumstances helpless men were found moving like weird shadows. Everything seemed terrifying. Returning to our newpaper office, I forgot to watch my watch. So I could not know what time it was. Ascended the stairs monotonously. In fact, I was agonised at that time and felt moribund.

With much confidence I handed over a piece of papar to our news editor. Because I had accepted his orders as a challenge. He read the paper and a ray of smile shone on his face. It evidenced his satisfaction. He raised his spectacles to the bridge of his nose and said, 'Excellent. Everything is ok. But if you add this line, it would magnify the hunger and grief. Inhabitants of the slum will eat withered spinach and moth-eaten brinjal if the relief carrying vehicle did not reach them.'

He opined in such a way that it seemed he himself had visited that place, seen Rebati. Not I but he had listened to her tale of woe and downcast with grief, he had given her another food-packet and a water bottle.

A little while before, I felt my lips had dried. Now my throat parched . When he himself wrote that line he did not appear ashmed. Nor did he try to hide his face. Of course he bent over the table a little because of years of experience like a butterfly of broken wings .

I looked at him without hesitation.

He wiped his lens and said, 'I feel terribly dejected and afraid after I saw that scene on Tv. How horrible and mangled I A train ran over the walking people returning from their distant working place at Howrah. Instantly all of them passed away. Bags, waterbottles and shirts soaked in blood lay beside the railway line.'

I couldn't count the stairs while descending; could n't recognise everyone - either known or unknown. Because all had put on masks. Strange, how the shape of face appears different so easily! Basu lost life in grief and tears when the pandemic spread, Could I relate this to Rebati?

Rebati might not have perused Fakirmohan's story. In case, she read, could she withstand such adversity? Could she control her tears? Not only for twenty - eight days, she will have to spend a solitary life throughout. Nobody would be there to clasp her to his or her bosom and caress her back. Who will realise this? Destiny or God?

How terrible mental agony is! Swallowing it I reached home. Load-sheddidng. Mother was sitting in the garden. It was a clear moonlit night. A whiff of air was blowing along the river of moonbeams. Who can swim across the river and go to the other side? The otherside does not suffer from Corona; there is happiness only.

At that strange moment someone asked in a dreamy tone, 'It's late. May be you are hungry?'

I couldn't look back. I felt snowy cold in my heart. Please convey this to none. Who can look back at the east direction of fear and terror?

Neither defeated nor Destroyed

Such a scene unthought of has created wonder and confusion. The bicycle has been kept leaning against the wall outside like an abandoned thing; a polythene bag has been hanging in a handle; the door was ajar and the threshold quite unpromising. Carrying a bag having sugar Sunita crossed the threshold and found Srikant sitting quite upset. He had forgotten to spread the mat. No article appeared preserved. The unsold *Sonapampdi* covered in a paper, was clearly visible from inside the glass jar kept beside the wall.

What's the reason of such paralysis of the entire environment? Even though she was present everything looked dispirited and mute in the faint light. Like a clock out of order. She looked here and there. Her son was in sound sleep. She perceived Srikant was looking at her for a long time to say something but in vain. He was not to return home so soon. It was time for business. Children, clad in clean dress, must be playing in the park; gas balloons tied to thread must be floating in the sky; under the star-studded sky must be sparkling the colourful park. And not finding Srikant at the particular spot, children must have returned disappointed.

Sonapampadi prepared by Srikant was soft and palatable. It would melt like costly and soft chocolates the moment it was put into mouth . Its taste was also quite special though it was a bit less sweet. That's why children used to crowd around his glass jar kept in the carrier. But why did Srikant return home so soon? Did he quarrell with any one or was he ill? She touched his forehead with her hand to know if he was ill. No, he didn't run a fever. Then what was the reason of his looking helpless like a cloudy sky? His muscles were tired, facial gestures abnormal. A patient person like him started crying. It was so pathetic that Sunita hugged him to her bosom.

- What's the matter? she asked.

Her frightened tone shook Srikant. He couldn't remember if he had heard such a tone before. His face appeared more tearful. He felt more anxiety-ridden.

'I am at my wit's end. Don't know what to do. Pray to God to let him live till I arrive there'- he said.

He raised his folded hands. He appeared possessed. Sunita asked again, 'Please, clarify what has happened. Othewise you would torment yourself.'

Her words showed him a way through darkness and solitariness as though. He gathered himself and said in an agonised tone, 'Father has been admitted into a nursing home three days back. He felt it difficult to breathe.'

It appeared all would stop - air in lungs, of heart palapitation and saline water streaming through a plastic pipe connected to these. Sunita had no difficulty to understand the problem. Except her body becoming inanimate.

She looked at his face. Though they saw each other's face, they remained in a fix - What step should they take at this crisis?

- What did you say? Father admitted into a nursing home! Her tone indicated that whatever she had heard was incomprehensible. A time comes in man's life when he thinks whatever he has heard is not true. It's false.

This thought made Sunita afraid. Then it disappeared. How could she believe this in this paralysed circumstance? It appeared things went out of control. What next? Could he not see father? Srikant sat straight as if he won't be defeated so soon by his mental agony and doubt.

- Tonight I shall journey by train - he said. Immediately his sense of helplessness vanished. He heaved a deep breath.

Now Sunita was sure, she had heard the truth. As true as darkness of night. She was sure there awaited an inevitable misery.

Srikant would journey by the train at 11O'clock night. No time to remain sad. He must reach the railway station by any means. A gush of wind entered the room like an assassin. Sunita drew the hem of her sari to her shoulder and asked, 'How can we - son and mother - manage here?' She was unable to express her mental agony fully in the teeth of such a stupendously impending danger. Her words remained half-expressed. Like the air getting obstructed. She felt breathless.

Unusual silence prevailed. Sunita had no courage to surmount such silence any more. She was sure Srikant's absence would destroy her existence even though the world would go on as usual. She did not know how she could manage herself in his absense. She would be paralysed.

Srikant leaned against the wall and stood up. In a bag he kept his pant, shirt, soap, tooth paste, brush and some coins. He was aware that within a short time he must reach the station. He had not booked a ticket. So he would do it at the counter. Thereafter, it won't be a problem even if he waited for the train for an hour. Because he would be sure he could catch the train and reach his village. And reach a seasoned person whose life was at stake.

He hang his bag on his shoulder, put on his chappal and said, 'Don't worry. I shall be back within seven days. Be watchful about our son. Don't let him go outside. I think the money in the trunk is sufficient to manage yourself for seven days. In case any difficulty arises, go to your father's house with son.'

Sunita was surprised because in spite of mental agony Srikant was concerned about her. However, she would live there alone and wait for his return.

She closed the unsafe door from inside. She was absent-minded and yet she smiled. She filled a silver plate with water, kept the glass box on it. *Sonpampadi* was kept in it rowwise. It had been closed by a wooden frame. Fully airtight. How can ants enter? Srikant, after returning from the park, used to keep the box carefully this way everyday. He would clean dust on it with his towel. So that his *sonpampadi* would be clearly visible from the transparent glass.

But they had a problem. They lived in a oneroom house. Cooking was being done on the verndah. The walls were greased with oil. Though the glass box looked clean, Sunita's face didn't look bright in the house. She was unable to demand a new piece of sari or a pair of silver anklets due to poverty. It was not a matter of yesterday or the day before yesterday. It had started since their marriage. Her father was unwilling for this. He was reluctant to give her in marriage to an ordinary person selling *sonpampad* beside road. Full of worries, he said, 'His home is far away. His whereabouts are unknown. Nobody knows what is in store for us. Suppose he quarrels with you and leaves for his house once for all, shall we not be disreputed? Moreover, he earns a meagre livelihood.'

Sunita protested, 'Yes, I agree with you. His house is far away. But are we so well off? If so, why do you stand in a queue in front of a grocery shop with your ration card every month?'

Father kept mum. Sunita's obduracy made him so. She also clearly saw how even today he felt awkward while meeting neighbours. Sunita had no relationshiop with her home anymore. The moment she brought with her the bicycle she had got from the governement while she was a school student, relationship ceased. The bicycle had remained unused after her departure. Dust had gathered on its seat and paddle. She was unable to read her name inscribed on the handle. But when she wiped it with a torn piece of cloth she could see her name. It had not yet rusted. The wheels were airless. When she dragged it outside, mother's eyes wet with tears, vanished behind walls. Her younger brother, taken aback, held the mudguard. But none pleaded with her to wait for a while;drink some water, sit silently; and things would be right. We would pump air into your cycle, grease its chain with oil. As a result, it would run smoothly as your own cycle.

It's a matter of regret, Srikant never realised its importance. As he used to live in a narrow house, swallowing all kinds of uncertainty he would feel shrunk easily. He would bend down with helplessness. Otherwise, he won't have said to her to go to father's house, she never remembered. Mother's eyes got bedimmed with tears. Father's affectionate voice too. Why should she remember the fullmoon night of relationship?

Why should she pine for her younger brother who said at that time, 'Apa, won't you really come any more?'

She became absent-minded and stared at the walls. She saw the long line of ants moving onward together. She was dumbfounded. Where were they - in the wall or under earth? Smelling *sonapampd* they came out to show their power. They would fight jointly in the teeth of any hindrance.

She fought with them till twelve at night -

But she encountered the real problem the day after. With whom she would leave her son? She was employed to do domestic chores in some families. In fact, she was averse to taking up such employment. She would feel breathless when she cleaned floors with phenyle. Its smell was extremely pungent. It churned the belly easily. However, she got habituated with it; she felt it no more now.

No more did she feel her hands tingled with burning sensation at the month's end. However, she knew this was no worse a misery in the world than poverty.

She hinged the door with a chain and locked it. Now her son, asleep on the mat, was safe. There was no possibility of his waking up. Undone, she was bound to bear the brunts born of uncontrollable circumstances. Otherwise, people would know she was bound in crisis. She also knew her crisis was temporary. So why should she worry? Only, she would be waiting for Srikant's return. It is wise on one's part not to reveal one's inability.

'I reached here with much difficulty'. After three days Srikant's voice was heard from the otherside in the morning. 'It was not so clear how I spent the night. Ticket was not available. So I did ticketless travel. Stood at the latrine door. Had to bribe. Yet father did not survive. Doctors failed.'

It created a confounding moment.

At times one sheds tears for someone whom one never saw, Sunanda's eyes glistened with tears. Wiping tears she asked, 'When are you returning?' The question indicated

Srikant's presence was urgent. In his absence things were in a position of stalemate. She could n't express it then.

- I shall inform when the obsequies are over. Sorry, here network doesn't function. You...

Sunita looked before the mirror and thought not to cry any more. Whether Srikant returned or not, son was with her. Her smiling face, now wet with tears, looked different. Everything was enveloped by darkness and tear.

After a couple of days as she opened her mistress's gate and was about to enter inside she heard something that startled her. Her legs stopped. She felt as if something broke upon her head.

-Why do you enter? Don't you know lock down has been declared? Don't come here anymore. You won't work anymore. Corona will spread here, if you come.'

Birds twittered in the branches of trees.

Sunita stood like a person suffering from an incurable disease. While the world was full of melody, how could she hear such a harsh and fearful shout? She couldn't understand.

She asked gently, 'How can I live if you stop me working?'

Similar was the reply, 'I can't say. Flee to your home, otherwise the police will arrest you.'

Perhaps madam was right. But she had least symptoms of that disease. She was annoyed and felt insulted too. Were Srikant there, she could have got some hints about the disease from him. He or she was there. Moreover, she was quite incapable of comprehending what lockdown was.

Srikant's mobile rang after about two hours. In a wearied voice, he asked, 'What do you say? I shall not be able to go back within seven days. From today trains will not run for twenty-one days. I shall tell you about my return when they start running again.'

Sunita leaned against the wall, quite dumbfounded. Said she, 'What's the matter? I don't know what the disease people are talking about. Madam prevented me from entering her house. Didn't allow me to work. I am at home. Quite bewildered. Money is almost exhausted.'

- Don't worry about money. I shall ask Sumanta to give you some. He belongs to our village. I shall take care of everything when I return. O Yes, wash your hands with soap again and again. Never go out. Don't let our child play with the neighbours' children. Corona is pandemic. Mask...

May be he wanted to speak something more. But the network did not work. The siren's honk produced more fear and terror . The police jeep moved along roads to caution all. Shops were locked. Schools and colleges were closed in no time. For social distancing circles in white colour were drawn. All wore masks. Even then the TV transmitted scenes of Corona. As a result, it created panic. It appeard a holocaust drew nigh.

Even after twenty-one days, the proclaimed lockdown was not lifted. It abnegated all possibilities. Srikant couldn't return. The second phase of lockdown had already started. It demanded more stringent security and control.

Sunita became impatient altogether.She was at her wit's end. Even though Sumanta had given money she had to borrow. She was startled like seeing a ghost,the moment the house owner stood before her residence and demanded the house rent. In fact, she had never imagined she would come across such a helpless moment. Another piece of information shook her completely - most residents of her locality were preparing to go back home because they were jobless there. There was no indication where work would be available. It was better if we left place for home than starve here. Let us face the eventuality.

Ten O'clock at night. Sumanta approached her and said, 'We will leave for home tomorrow morning. We have decided it is better to go to our village than starve here. Will you come with us?'

May be she was waiting for such a moment. 'How long could I sustain myself and son this way? No more. Srikant also was uncertain about his return. I could not hide myself as I was unable to pay the house rent yesterday I was compelled to sell the bicycle to pay the house rent. The house owner threatened if I delayed payment of the house rent, next month, he would lock the house.'

A person in this situation needs shelter and faith.Somebody may extend help, give consolation. But she didn't get that. Srikant stayed put there as vehicles didn't ply. She found nobody here who would say, 'Be not afraid. I am for you. Come what may, you will not be lost.'

For the first time she experienced how night dawned with so much gratitude. She inhaled the fragrance of some anonymous flower.

The eastern horizon became slightly red. The sun rose signalling all possibilities as it were. Indeed man is undaunted and imperishable. An unprecedented scene she witnessed while she approached the National Highway by her bicycle.

Human beings were walking beside the road in the midst of colossal disarrangement. Come what may, it was very urgent for them to reach their respective villages. Because they had some kith and kin there. And she would caress them and express emotionally a word of cosolation. He or she could swallow their grief.

The police in front stopped Sunita from going, 'Where are you going at this lockdown period?' he asked.

Her son looked like luggage on her back. The child was not even one year old. He looked at the distant sky where the red sun shone like a deep red orange. His face had half cherubic smile. One day he would go to school. Like other children he would study there and be man. Growing up he could not know one day he had crossed a long way of hurdle being huddled like a luggage on his mother's back . Could Sunita broach this to him? Never. The child's face shone with a smile of red power. The smile got scattered in Sunita's heart like the petals of a flower. She felt energised, and said confidently, 'Darabhanga'.

The policeman trembled in fear and handed a packet of food, a bottle of water and a mask over to her. Perhaps he was not certain about how distant Darabhanga was and how much time it would take to reach there. Sunita realised this and chuckled for a while. She was confident, none in the way could obstruct her. Her inexperienced legs had gathered all strength of the world. Her hands remained steady on the handle; her back, slightly bent,carried the burden of the entire world. She turned herself into an ant to carry the burden. On the carrier was the glassbox of *sonpampd* that resembled Alladin's lamp. Innumerable ants forming a line were running onward behind it.

Sunita, if asked by anyone in the world at this moment, would not hesitate to give her whereabouts briefly. From such adventure she realised man's hunger, sorrow and disease are not everlasting.

The Unmanifest

Darkness on the banks of the river Gobari; darkness beneath water, the fog was as dark as darkness. The darkness hid tears and pathos. A strange time. The boat at the otherside of the river was heard through the darkness. The ferryman and the oar were not present. Yet the boat was ashore. 'It would not be pre-dawn. The wind would have been still, low and agreeable note of birds would not be heard; no indication of movement would be got through thick foliage; an uninterrupted sacred hymnal sound would be coming - these constitute an early dawn of gods, when the creation chants mantra. I assure you to come back at this moment.'

Expressing an undefinable statement, the graceful person got into the boat a saintly person with a sandal paste mark on forehead.

A very startling environment indeed.

He had vanished. None knew where - whether in the river bed or in the sky.

A few villagers present there felt a spiritual force. Then they loitered here and there, returned to the village, witnessed another scene that astounded them. None of them uttered a single word. May be words had forgotten their form. What happened? A corpse under a clean and white piece of cloth kept on the village road. However, sandal paste and a burning earthen lamp were there. The sound of the *mridanga* appeared to be a silent prayer.

Impossible to meet Shraddhananda alive. The sound of his wooden sandals would scare goblins, ghosts of a Brahmin who died a bachelor. So they dared not enter the village. One such ghost, unware of his power, tormented all on the village road. It used to torment people returning from Kolkota by that way as if the public grazing field belonged to it entirely. It is said some people had met it. Shraddhanada got the information. Nobody knew what was the time then at night. The sound of his wooden sandals pounded like slabs of stone. Even stray dogs got scared and hid themselves beside stacks of straw. Since then the ghost was found nowhere. It was made a captive on the palm tree and the mischievous lost its freedom. It would be shaky in unusually stormy nights. the boughs of the palm tree, rattling its teeth. Dust would fall off foliage. However, nobody reported that he had met it. Because it had lost its power to descend from the tree since that night. That's why the tailor bird never built its nest on that particular tree.

This may sound to be an extra terrestrial story. But in my childhood I heard it from grandmother. Of course, she had not seen Shraddhananda. But whenver she narrated, it seemed she had seen him and heard his voice - the voice that had imprisoned the ghost on the tree till then. Even though the boughs of the palm tree were about to fall, these kept hanging, awaiting the dawn of a possibility. That Sraddhananda would return. And it would be free at an unguarded moment.

A small village on the river Gobari that flowed beside it. There were rows of thatched houses, having raised platforms on which holy *Basil* plants had been planted. A village pathasala was there. The teacher used to teach the pupils alphabet on a slate using a big lump of chalk. His finger would bear the mark of chalk powder which he used to wash in water.

There was a temple adjacent to the village pathasala. The *goddess* of the village had been consecrated here. Cymbals and bells are sounded here every morning and evening. Sometimes the priest Nira stops worshipping the goddess. Nobody knows why. But somehow the reason comes out. One day the priest's family remains starved. Our grandmother makes a packet of plantain leaves, puts rice, dal and brinjal sauce in it and sends it to his house through me. His dilapidated house is situated after four to five houses. His children surround me as they see the bundle in my hand. Niranana relishes the food and asks, 'Has sister sent betel ? Very tasty . If one chews it one's mouth will smell for a considerable time.'

This way the village continues living with many beliefs and so much love.

Sister Nakhi approaches grandmother when her catechu is exhausted. She takes excessive catechu so that her tongue turns red. She moves it this side and that and says, 'My mouth was dry. Because of your lump of catechu it turned watery. Nowhere one can find such sweet smelling catechu. Even Dina does not sell it. He sells not genuine articles brought from Kolkata. If someone points it out, he would hiss like a cobra-de-capella.' After a pause he would say, 'Give me fragance. I haven't tasted it since long.'

Grandmother would slowly cut muristica fragrance with her nut-cracker. So that no portion of it would fall on the floor. Immediately sister Nikhi would throw it into her mouth; she would sit for some time, would never spit even a small bit of it on the ground. While leaving she would take with her sweet potato and dillenia speciosa and sweet balls of sesam for her granddaughter. She would preserve all these as precious wealth. At times she would give me one. Then she would say to sister Nakhi, 'Touch your hand on my grandson's head, bless him. He will study well, be reputed and marry an incomparable damsel.'

As I hear it, I feel ashamed and rush outside. Stand beside Sunita, learning against the moonbeam tree. Sunita is sister Nakhi's daughter, seven years younger than me. She wears a tattered frock and waits for Nakhinana. Other girls used to play the game of ducks and drakes. No more in vogue is the game.

The village has changed. Its muddy road has been transformed into a concrete one. Water now flows spontaneously the moment water tap is moved. The school building in place of the village *pathasala* stands on the village square. No more one sees mats of palm leaves. Pupils are getting admitted to school straightway. There is no caning any more there. Midday meal system has been introduced in the school. Pupils are being provided text books free of cost.

Shankar, Dina's son is in charge of his betel shop. A tender youngman, he combs his hair backside with a comb he has kept inhis pocket. Wears black goggles and sports a brass bangle. Brings 'Dilkhus' betel spice from Cuttack. He chews betel leaves that add 'Baba' tobacco. He sells 'gutkas' that shine from his shop. Sells wine in secret.

People no more go to Kolkata to earn their livelihood. Dilu Mian - His eyes looked as red as the china rose. Deep red. Wearing a lungi, he used to come from Kendrapada, tying a goat to her cycle carrier. Meat would be sold on plantain leaves. When father was alive, he used to bring meat to our house. Of course, in those days meat was pohibited entry into our house. A hearth was there at the backside of our house. At the end of the place where there was threshing horse, it was being cooked in a silver pan. She never allowed its fleshy smell to enter inside the house. Grandmother would wash the floor, verndah and prayer room. Mother would keep silent. But grandma would be irritated if I strolled along the wet verndah. She would shout - Go away, otherwise you will catch cold.

Now his son in law Kalu Mian has opened his meat shop in our village. A tin-roofed place where there was a log of wood. He used to butcher goats there . He could spell out how old the goat was just by touching it with his finger . While butchering a healthy goat, his hand would never tremble. May be he thought he was not cutting the neck of the goat, rather a smooth plantain leaf. One can feel the tragedy of death if one is concerned about life. A man holding a sharp knife is abjectly unable to feel whose neck it cuts. So very easily he catches hold of the goat's ear and says, 'Very soft, it would taste sweet. Really very young.'

Grandmother lay in bed for a month and then passed away. Father followed her. When he was eager to listen to a word, his breathing stopped. His face looked quite different on his death bed.

We performed obsequies at the village. Our kith and kin were satisfied and returned to Cuttack after fifteen days. But mother did not accompany me. She urged to stay in the village, 'I shall stay here.'

Her utterance ramained incomprehensible. God knows why man is reluctant to give up his prolonged grief. Even if he has nothing, he thinks, he has everything. Perhaps this is 'Maya' (illusion)

What is the feature of 'Maya'? I can't say, But this much I know everything can be abandoned. When you can leave your body, if you are worried about ephemeral objects you will simply swallow pain and nothing but pain. This reality is the Gordian Knot.

Like grandmother, mother washes our prayer room everyday because she has interest, curiosity and fear of life. She decorates the deity's head with moonbeam flowers. She washes the raised platform pouring water profusely. And with unlimited faith too.

She rang me two days back. Said very gently, 'A miracle has taken place.'

Her silence appeared more errie. She was so agitated that she was unable to express herself. In a low tone she said, 'The deity Sraddhananda has made his advent at the wild fig tree which the priest Nakhinana used to worship. He has possessed Sunita and is issuing divine ordinancne. He prescribes ways more than necessary to cure diseases. Hundreds of people from distant places are thronging the place. By his grace they come round. Come with Sunanda; she suffers from colic...'

Her words remained incomplete. But it was evident she was woebegone for Sunanda. It's a fact Sunanda was suffering for a longtime. At times she would get senseless because of her abdominal colic pain. All treatment has proved fruitless. But when doctors say she is all right, I feel surprised. If that is so, then why is she suffering? Very puzzling indeed.

I don't believe Sunanda will be cured by any miraculous power. But as she heard mother, she said, 'Let's go,'

Nobody knows how at times intricate problems are solved so easily. Such as a snake bitten fellow walking. Villagers had witnessed so many astounding scenes, like this. A red flag and bracelets made of conchshell was tied to a branch of the wild-fig here. At its feet was a heap of earth which resembled a human face. It was fenced by a screen of bamboo laths. Now it yields rare fruits. There lay prostrate reverentially many diseased and grief-stricken fellows.

Sunita was in a meditating pose. A vermilion mark on her forehead shone brightly. She was clad in a red saree. Her eyes were brighter. She had embellished herself as a goddess.

Her face reflected amazing brilliance.

I felt surprised . I could not remember at all the face of the girl putting on a tattered frock.

I knew vast wealth was waiting for her. She used to take a ball of sweet made from sesame from Nakhi sister's hand, gulp it down at once and chew and derive much delight. The same sort of delight she nursed in her now. Perhaps she was in quest of happiness and delight.

As she saw Sunanda, she turned grave. Without a word, she gave her a root. She raised her hand in a benedictory gesture and muttered something which she herself might not have heard. The sound of cymbals and balls drowned all this. She threw a bunch of flowers on Sunanda.

A ripe leaf fell on the ground.

It created a weird atmosphere.

While jostling through the crowd, I saw Sunanda's face bore signs of apathy. She pressed her teeth slowly and hardened her palm on my shoulder.

Her pain started again. It was unbearable . She wanted to sit somewhere to alleviate pain. Drops of sweat gathered on her nape and forehead.

The wind blew slowly. There stood tall palm trees, and at a short distance there were Pandanis bushes.

In a temporary shop, a child cried. Sunanda sat there

in a chair, pressing her belly. Tears trickled down her eyes.

Wearing black goggles, Shankar came to us and asked, 'Do you suffer from colic? May be due to gas. It will go away if you take a cold drink.'

But Sunanda declined. She pressed her belly and stared at the top of the palm tree. 'O God! Am I so unfortunate. So much sorrow for me.'

She asked as if someone were there.

The palm tree appeared to be becoming unusually taller. I turned my attention to Shankar and asked, 'How is your business here?'

- Roaring. Unable to supply commodities. My stock today gets exhausted today. The shop remains empty. Please see, how commodities are being carried by truck. Straight from godowns. All this due to the miraculous power of Shraddhanda. Within a few days our village would turn into a town.'

He may be betel shopkeeper Dina's son but his words carried weight. His golden necklace sparkled. He may have known of its weight. But that appeared weighty as it had created a scar around his neck.

He came to me and said, 'Everyone is lucky here. People are earning according to their opportunistic stance. Heaps of commodities have gathered in the village. A film hall will be built. Therefore plans are afoot to fell palmtrees. So the rate of land here will be exorbitant.'

Sunanda was reluctant to be there for long. Her pain had decreased to some extent. She washed her face with a handful of water and wiped the dripping water with her handkerchief. She looked fresh but looked at me blankly. She was not eager even to utter a word. Perhaps some groundless sorrow ramained suppressed in her.

She didn't take anything at night.

Entered the prayer room before going to bed. Sat silently there.

I was quite puzzled if by any other means she could come round. That root was in my pocket. She also paid no attention to it. Mother had put fine unparboiled rice, some black gram and vegetables produced in our orchard. She had also packed papaya in a separate bag. It became ripe within one or two days.

Sunanda touched her feet reverntially. Mother's eyes were brimful with tears.

'Grind the root and take, I feel you will come round this time' said she.

Full of credulity, she caressed Sunanda with her weak hands.

Our vehicle ran onward. It was not yet dawn. The path was not visible because of fog. The air was unmoved in the midst of foliage. Darkness enveloped everywhere.

Our vehicle may have crossed a little distance when Sunanda said, 'Please stop the vehicle. I feel acute pain in my stomach. Quite unbearable. What shall I do?'

We stopped on the banks of the river Gobari. I opened the door and came out. Sunanda followed me and stood leaning against me. Her hands were getting tightened. Splashing in water was heard.

A bicycle bell indicated someone was coming through the fog, dispelling darkness. As the cycle stopped in my front, I recognised he was Kalu Mian.

- Sir, are you returning to Cuttack? He asked.

Answered I, 'Yes, but where are you going at such late hours of night?'

He wiped his face wet in fog and said, 'Here all business stands still. Meat is prohibited in the village. So I am going to Kendrapada to do my butchery there. One must earn one's livelihood.' His words betrayed his disappointment. May be there was a hungry knife in his bag. He was at his wit's end what to do. When he was unable to sustain himself, it was useless to think of the knife.

He disappeared through the fog.

Sunanda shouted in an incredible tone, 'See, someone covered with a white piece of cloth walking on water there.'

Was it possible - somebody walking on water like a phatom! Her words sounded mysterious. But I could not see that scene. Because there was fog all around. May be it was her illusion . May be she saw in her sleepy eyes such a scene as she had not a wink of sleep at night.

Only splashing of water was being heard.

She came close to me and said slowly, 'I have been trying for so many days to speak to you something, but in vain. I am afraid, I feel shattered in my heart of hearts.'

I drew her to me, caressed her face that shone in innocence. The cold wind blew from the eastern direction, low and agreeable notes of birds were heard.

Sunanda looked at the full river and said, 'May be the boy was fourteen or fifteen. He was reading with me in class ten. Quite lanky he was. But I enjoyed his sweet talks. One day, while giving me his note, he had placed his hands on my abdomen. Without his knowledge.

I felt my body getting poisoned. Who could I breach the matter to? I was haunted with evil thoughts. Since then I have been suffering form pain. Just on the same spot in my abdomen.'

She could speak no more and started sobbing.

A strange piece of news from our village reached us after about a week . We believed it to be true. Sunita was no more in the village. She had eloped with Shankar to Surat. That saree of red colour was hanging like a bird on the branches of the wild fig tree. With it was flying the flag.

The plan afoot to fell the palm tree to construct a cinema hall had been stopped. No more was there any crowd . The truck carrying goods from the godown was running in a different direction. On day time foxe's yelp was being heard among screwpine bushes.

Soundless had become the surroundings of the wild fig tree.

The ghost has remained imprisoned in the palm tree. At times it would shake the boughs of the tree. It would thump its legs but would be unable to descend. Had the palm tree been felled, it would have been free at any unguarded moment.

But that was not possible.

But the most wonderful matter was, after returning from the village Sunanda suffered from no colic pain any more. She was totally cured.

The silent, lonely and lifeless banks of the river Gobari remained more mysterious. None walked on water that day, nobody's face was reflectd in water too.

The Infection

Strange was the dawn in the month of *Chaitra*. As if fire circumambulated the body and bed. Flowers bloomed in the mind like bright stars. The zephyr played hide and seek through the window. The hapless home and hunger embraced such a romantic moment.

The split wall was visible through darkness. The plank of the door tottered though, it had a chain.

Kamala woke up leaning on hands. No more was it possible on her part to stand up. She wished to enjoy a sound sleep. She won't wake up even if someone called her loudly. She was not interesed to know if any woman on her family way for seven months would be waking up so early in the morning.

Somehow she approached the door; washed her face with water from an earthen pot. She took a glance at her disfigured face in the broken mirror placed at a niche.

She put on a red *bindi* on her brow. Her face glistened.

- Hello, won't you go for the master's household work? See, the sun is already up adequately. What are you doing inside house? You won't be coming out of house, if Sania were there?'

Kamala shrank in shame. But where was Sania? But his face would appear through darkness to satiate her mental hunger. Not possible to embrace him in broad day light.

Her overwhelming satiety and emotion got blended in her body.

She closed the door.

Auntie Rama stood beside the verndha. She smiled, caressed Kamala's belly and asked, 'How many months to go?'

Her tears surpassed her sorrow. Drops of tears welled up in her eyes. She was at her wit's end. She cast a foolish glance at Rama auntie. In spite of unwillingness, she licked her tongue on her dry lips.She was weak.

Her whole being got shrunk. She lost mental power - 'All right. You may not divulge. But be careful, while walking. See, a child must be playing in your lap by the time Sania arrives.'

An easy moment then. Kamala chuckled, though her condition was precarious.

She said, 'Three more months. Yet it has started pressing its legs to come out.'

The myna at the bush flew towards paddy fields. It was a season of leaves falling off trees. Dry leaves would fall with a pinch of disappointment. Trees would look bald. Grey would be the earth. New tendrils would sprout to envisage such condition. Hence trees would turn green. Every nook and corner of the earth would be filled with rain water. Cultivation would start. But how far was the month of *Asadha*?

Sania had promised to return in the month of *Asadha*.

Kamala was ignorant of the demands and necessities of life with which one lived. But this much she knew - the spilt walls would be plastered; the thatched roof would be repaired; Sania would repay the debt of two thousand rupees when he returned.

But things no more went as gay as before. She was getting overwhemled with grief.

Grief might melt if tears were wiped. But how could hunger?

She stood at the master's door from early dawn. Only to earn two dry loaves of bread. Quite helplessly and shamelessly.

- Come, after finishing duties - Auntie Rama said almost in a supplicating tone.

But where? Perhaps Kamala could not know. She wondered for what important work auntie requested her so .

For the moment time stood still.

- Well, come to the bamboo garden. Dry leaves have fallen there. Might be burnt to ashes if someone set fire to it. The mistress said, 'If you collect those leaves with a broom, she would give its half.'

Auntie Rama's words were a challenge, as it were. She had seen such scenes during competitions in her school days. A line of demarcation drawn in white powder was there. A *jalebi* tied to thread was hanging at a distance of one hundred meters. The race started when the whistle was blown. Runners never thought of their sweating bodies. Moreover, their legs got tired. Yet who could jump forcefully? Yet the *jilabi* kept undiminished wonder still.

How many times had she not jumped! But her lips failed even to touch one fourth ot that *jilabi*. It's in vain to pine for happiness in this life. She knew she would live this way.

- Auntie, you see my condition. How can I do that?

Kamala had lost self-confidence and courage. In fact, in adversity all break down like this. He or she finds no way out.

Rama auntie wondered. To inspire her, she said, 'See, you won't worry any more for fuels for three months.'

Life had already become stalemate. At times she cooked a little. If one day she did it, on the other day she had nothing. Hence her hearth remained unlit.

What was needed first - rice or fuel?

Kamala could not be conscious to get an answer to this.

Indeed, an unbearable situation. She knew the night of her struggle for existence won't be over so soon.

Someone paddling a bicycle and blowing horn appeared to have brushed past her. Kamala failed to recognise him,.

She felt losing patience day by day and her mind getting assailed by fear. The situation is getting precipitated.

She looked around, quited baffled.

A channel road ran in the midst of screwpine bushes and pagoda trees. A dillenia specicosa tree had hung towards it. An unkown bird was brushing its beak on its branch.

The soft sun had scattered along the roof. There was a cowshed; a tub near it, there were some plates used for taking food. A well was there on the otherside of the tub. Without anybody's order, a can tied to a rope would be dropped into the well. Without having any desire for reaping fruit. Though the well had enough water, it was not sufficient to quench Kamala's thirst after plates were cleaned. She would look into the house pathetically and anxiously.

She would be speechless, expressing gratefulness to the entire world.

At this moment the superb smell of stale curry along with two loaves of bread would indicate perhaps it was enough to satisfy her world.

What more should a famished one desire? Hence he/she would fold his/her hands to the sympathetic person who offered the moment.

The mistress's face would appear behind the door. She would ask, 'Want tea?'

Such an intimate voice would clasp her like a little girl. Habitulally she would ask, 'Is there biscuit? Very smooth to chew, salty too. It gets melted the moment it is put into mouth.'

May be a harsh voice snarled. The rope slipped off hands; the can flung into the well.

Kamala turned back. She felt shurnk inside. In fear she failed to fathom what happened. May be she committed some mistake unknowingly. Due to her inattentiveness the stray dog licked the plates used for taking food. Certainly.

- What are you doing?

- Drawing water - Kamala said gently.

- What do you say? Drawing water, when the can had fallen into the well! Get out. No need of washing plates from today - the master fumed.

The sky was not visible anymore. The wind stood still. The mistress didn't offer her two loaves of bread that looked like the moon. Why was the master so furious? Because she declined to gather dried leaves using a broom, he said so. Let it be, I shall obey what he ordered.

Of course it was unbearbale when the child pushed its legs inside the belly. Yet I shall tightly tie a towel around my waist, sweep dried leaves and gather those. The mistress was as generous as mother Luxmi. How could I transgress her?

Strange! the mistress's face was no more visible through the door!

- Where do you look at? Mother won't come out any more. You don't know - lockdown has been clamped. Nobody would come out.

The master's face did not appear familiar; his words too sounded incomprehensible.

Even he didn't look at the red *bindi* she had put on so beautifully.

A very comely morning of soft sunshine. A crow cawed on the roof. Enough time there was for sunshines to become hard.

- Well , why do you stare? Be off immediately and go to your house. Last night the news said markets, bazars would remain shut. Nobody should visit anybody's house. Children should not attend school.'

The situation was so complicated for Kamala to grasp its intricacy. Gradually she was setting by a moment of conflict and reaction lesseness. Disappointment and affliction were visible on her brow. While coming to the master's house, she thought to pluck two or three spinachs while cleaning the master's yard.

She would add it to the insufficient rice she had and make it her lunch.

Alas! another type of scene awaited her here.

She heaved a deep sigh.

- Sin skyrocketed. How much of it could the earth bear? Man ate bats, snakes, worms, etc. So now diseases are aplenty. So much suffering. None can get away from the wrath of Providence. The Corona virus has set a trap of death.

Disconnected utterances - aimless.

The master came to the well, looked vigilantly at the plates kept to be washed and returned angrily.

Kamala felt unusual discontent and anger. An unknown fear hovered around the well. She turned impatient, wiped her wet hand, with the hem of her saree and inattentively walked along the channel way to her home.

The *champak* flower plant had not borne yellow flowers till now.

She had forgotten to bolt the door of her house. The door was getting dashed by the wind. May be stray dogs had entered the house and licked here and there. There was nothing with which they could satisfy their hunger. Not even a morsel of rice in the earthen bowl.

Hunger and hunger everywhere - the map of hunger only.

While bringing a basket from inside the house, Kamal's hands trembled like the hands of an epileptic. A mild headache she felt. How rare have become moments without hunger!

She drank three draughts of water and came out of her house. Her plot of greens had withered. Its green leaves had almost withered. It stood shorn of branches. While Sania was present here, he used to water it profusely. Really incredible. Indeed he knew magic. He would deweed the plot and water. it.

Lo, tender green leaves would blossom from the lopped off branches to offer vast treasure. The smell of spinach would make the house fragrant thrice or four times a week.

It was an uncontrollable moment for her.

The sun moved to the middle of the sky. Very scorching sunshine. Her house appeared extremely suffocating. Her fortune. She wiped her face by her sweating palm. Her face looked deplorable.

Shadowy darkness enveloped inside the basket.

The lanky Banamber moved his bicycle and approached her. He had wound a towel around his head. With more keenness, he said, 'How is Sania? He has left the village almost before six to seven months. And what about my money?'

After a little pause, Kamala said in a low voice, 'You know he went after *Dasahara*. Only because you gave money. Otherwise how could he have gone to Hyderabad - so distant a place? Needed much fare. He went there with our villagers hoping to earn more wages.'

- Do you speak the truth he will earn more wages there? But even during the three to four months he didn't send money. I warn you, I shall charge compound interest after the month of *Chaitra*.

More distressed looked the plot of spinach. The house too.

- He would repay your money with interest when he comes back- said she.

At times she would feel mentally strong, perceive the earth beneath her feet more solid, more protective.

Banamber took a few steps onward, looked back and said, 'Not easy to return. Buses, trains would not run for twenty-one days. Everyone would stay put. No more would the factories remain functioning. Employment would not be available. If anyone returns , villagers won't allow him access to village so easily.'

Kamala's hands and legs turned cold. How could Banamber say such mind-boggling words? How could she feed herself in the event of nonavailability of employment? How could she survive? No, it's a blatant lie-his hypocrisy to realise more interest.

While Banamber paced onward, paddling his bicycle, he looked back once again. It did't appear to be his naive conduct. He cast his glance again and again not at Kamala's brow but at her bulging belly of seven months. The belly admitted unwillingly the unprecedented flow of the mysteries of life.

Surprised, Kamala moved her hand around her belly, hid it from the assassin's view and moved onward.

Now she also forgot to enchain the door. Hence the door remained open as before.

A bud through the leaves of the *champak* flower tree showed itself a little. It saw the world. The cuckoo cooed from the branches of the dillenia speciosa tree.

Kamala walked along the way wearily. As if, she carried herself. Drops of sweat rose on her brow and neck. The hot wind emitted steam.

She found none at the well, knocked at the back door. The door opened producing a little sound. The mistress stood in her front. She said haltingly, 'Well, you left even while I was coming to you. I enquired of you after you left. Well, what have you taken?'

Kamala was about to cry.

A handful of sweet fried rice streamed on the corner of her saree. - Well, take it first and then drink some water. Your condition is so unbearble. How could you come here in the scorching sun?

A sensation spread in her blood vessels because of such consolation. A handful of sweetened fried rice sweetened her mouth. It tasted like nectar. She sipped a glass of water and asked, 'Is communication stopped from today? Mother, you watch TV; Please tell me the truth. I don't believe in what Banamber says.'

She took another handful of sweetened fried rice. She felt, hunger was not invincible. The most important matter was to keep on living. Even in the teeth of hunger and adversity.

- His words are not white lies. The pandemic is spreadig. So, such restrications. You won't have to wash untensils. Instead you would do another piece of work. The mistress indicated something by her eyes.

- Could I do it? Kamala asked very gently.

Said the mistress, there are about ten to twelve mango trees beside your house. You know, Makara used to guard those. But he would act as a guard at the end of the village. He would hand over soap and water jug to anyone who visited the village. So all would wash their hands and then enter the village. That duty would be better than keeping a constant vigil on mango trees. They said. But you will guard mango trees. I shall pay you one thousand rupees. Do you agree?"

Kamala was startled - one thousand rupees to keep vigil on twelve mangeo trees! Her eyes closed in bliss. The child in her womb turned sides. As if, it encouraged her; this much was enough for her! She didn't express her delight. However, keeping a vigil on the mango trees was not that easy. Everything would be damaged if a herd of mankeys entered. And then the master was of such nature he won't pay a pice.

- What do you think? Only for a month. I shall give you vegetables along with rice. You will have to guard the trees. O, yes, there is a hut; you would stay inside it. You told me you had no ration card. I shall get you this through your master. Government have announced to supply in advance rice for three months.'

So much dream at a moment! Not dream, in reality she poured into the corner of Kamala's saree , rice, some potatoes, two brinjals and one ripe papeya.

- Listen, take an earthen pot there. You will cook there.

The mistress's assurance drove her fear and hunger away. She failed to see the picture of the spread of the pandemic. While TVs were discussing such an adversity, she started preparing a hut of straw and bamboo. Also a hearth and put rice, potato, brinjal in it, filled it with water, too.

The water started boiling; rice and vegetables got boiled. She poured the steaming rice on a plantain leaf. The steam of the boiled rice indicated everything was ok now.

A squirrel was playing. An unkown bird was flapping its wings, a very strange and incredible appearance, the mango grove assured.

Sania was far, far away at Hyderabad. But he stood beside her the moment she closed her eyes . Like a mango tree, he would embrace her lowering the branches, as it were. Didn't matter where he was - at home or outside - he was beside her . He was her strength and courage. Otherwise, how could she have remained awake fearlessly inside the hut and guarded the mango grove!

It's not easy to recognise a man from his face. A face was seen near the hut in the darkness of night. How terrible! Kamala shouted - who is there? Who?

With a staff in her hand, she stood at the hut's door and hear footsteps running along the canal way.

This way she passed twenty days.

Green mangoes smiled with ripeness. Cooing of the cuckoo indicated it was time to return.

Overwhelmed, she counted the mangoes. Nobody had courage to steal even a single mango. Because of her strict vigil. She moved her hand all around her bulging belly. Experienced more happiness, more delight.

Just then an incredible piece of news spread throughout the village. The entire village woke up in the dark night. None could comprehend how he could cover such a long distance! That too on a bicycle?

Rama auntie fell from the heaven - who can be so mad to do this!

She whispered in Kamala's ear, 'Sonia has fled

Hyderbad. Riding a bicycle. Villagers won't allow him to enter the village. He would stay at the school building for fourteen days. For, he may have carried that disease with him.'

Kamala took long time to understand what it meant.

Darkness. Darkness all around. The moon had already set. A staff in hand, Kamala walked silently along the embankment of the tank. Noone was awake in the dark night to recognise her.

Very intimate experience - soft wind blew to touch one's mind.

The school boundary. Anyone who came would stop there. Inside, there were cots, clean bedsheets, glasses of water; fans whirring. Makara kept a strict vigil on the otherside of the boundary.

- Who is there? Who? - He shouted.

Kamala could not reply. She turned back and started running - on the way or off the way? Though she had held a staff in her hand, she fell down along the zigzag path. May be one aim of life is to cross a difficult road. Kamala competed with herself. There was no *jilabi* tied to a string and hanging. Yet she ran and ran. Her legs trembled. Her destination was unknown.

She fell on her bed inside the hut. Her saree was no longer on her body. Her body was wet with sweat and dust. She had lost the staff somewhere. Not possible to know in darkness.

The dawn was approaching. Prognosticating all possibilities, the eastern sky was getting clearer.

Darkened redness got scattered throughout the sky. Mango trees looked jaded; the environment was ruffled - leaves plucked, ripe mangoes stolen, saps oozing from stalks. Who committed such crime? Strange, the whole surroundings were destroyed even in absence for an hour! One's future impoverished.

All doors in the world were shut - Kamala did not know the door through which she could get out.

She was counting one, two three, four, five...her eyes closed. At this hour the breathless master reached. He was accompanied by three to four persons - all perturbed and thoughtful. He said, 'I knew such would happen. Who can control one's greed for *Amropalli* mangoes? Leave it. After all she is a woman. She was out to visit Sania last night. Makar saw this. First put her in quarantine; test her swab, otherwise the corona virus would infect the entire village. None would be cured of that disease.'

Kamala lost consciousness in the midst of the crowd. Not for the corona virus but due to the infection of the virus of starvation. For two days, her inner world had turned dark, as it were! Her mouth had turned sticky.

Whose face was visible in darkness? What was his name? His whereabouts? Could this be asked to any one? Rama auntie sprinkled a handful of water on Kamala's face and said, 'Hey, for us a disease and hunger are similar. No use to lie unconscious. Open eyes. For the child...'

The shadow of the flying golden oriole was seen no more.

Kamala rose slowly. The shadow of her body looked like the golden oriole on the ground. No more fear. Now she could traverse the unending path of the struggle of life.

BLACK EAGLE BOOKS

www.blackeaglebooks.org
info@blackeaglebooks.org

Black Eagle Books, an independent publisher, was founded as a nonprofit organization in April, 2019. It is our mission to connect and engage the Indian diaspora and the world at large with the best of works of world literature published on a collaborative platform, with special emphasis on foregrounding Contemporary Classics and New Writing.